YOUR MOTHER'S NIGHTMARES

ANITHA KRISHNAN

DREAM PEDLAR BOOKS

Ebook ISBN: 978-1-7388158-9-0

Paperback ISBN: 978-1-998472-00-0

Cover stock image 'Vector illustration of a girl with a balloon in black silhouette' by ThemesSO (Marek Tyczyński) on Depositphotos; Standard License purchased on 31 August 2023

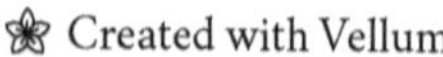 Created with Vellum

For Dhruv,
the greatest miracle in my life.

Just the sight of you makes my world so much brighter that even the
darkest nightmares simply fade away.

Thank you for coming into my life.

ABOUT THIS BOOK

Your Mother's Nightmares

The worst is not what happens.
The worst is what every mother fears could happen.

Imagination collides with maternal fear in this bold collection
of troubling, twisted tales from a fiction writer who isn't
afraid to plumb the often terrifying emotional depths of the
motherhood experience.

A party across the street lures a trusting three-year-old into
an adventure, but thrusts his mother into a nightmare.

A mirror offers the gift of more time, something every parent
longs for, but what will it take in return?

A mother erases her seven-year-old's painful memories to

leave him with the impression of a perfect childhood. Only, it leads to imperfect consequences.

Teeming with the unthinkable, this collection of six never-before-seen short stories tugs at every mother's helpless heartstrings, coaxes out her deepest and darkest fears for her children, and presents them in the guise of fantasy fiction so that her nightmares won't come true.

Stories included are:
The Party across the Street
A Suitable Colour for a Ghost
*Memory Games**
The Goldilocks Zone
*Hide-and-Seek***
The Gift of Time

Memory Games secured an Honourable Mention in the L. Ron Hubbard Writers of the Future Contest, July—September 2023 quarter.

**Hide-and-Seek secured an Honourable Mention in the Spring/Summer 2021 issue of Allegory Magazine, Volume 39/66.*

Dear Reader,

Motherhood, or even parenting in general, is one of those life experiences that are almost universal yet remarkably unique to each one of us.

Everyone's parenting journey is vastly different. What works for one parent/family may simply not work for another.

My own journey has been a mix of unimaginable joys and unbelievable anxieties and everything else in between these two extremes.

During those dark moments, I turned to writing as a salve. I couldn't bring myself to speak aloud the fears I had for my child. Already wracked with anxiety and a deep sense of wrongness for even having those fears in the first place, I was terrified that putting them in written or spoken form—by journalling or talking about them to someone—might just make them come true.

Instead, I couched them in the guise of speculative fiction to render them more palatable, more surmountable, and as a reminder that in those moments my fears were exactly that—fiction!

It's for this very reason that I now present this collection to you.

If you're a parent, my hope is that in these pages, you too will find the words for the darkness you already know so intimately and grapple with every single day, and emerge into the light on the other side, feeling seen and sane and safe in the knowledge that you are doing the best you can and that is more than enough.

~ Anitha Krishnan
Burlington, Ontario,
Wednesday, 17 April 2024

THE PARTY ACROSS THE STREET

THE PARTY ACROSS THE STREET

When the house across the street swallows up a visitor dressed for a party at 1 a.m., three-year-old Dorian is curious to know more.

Excited at the prospect of an entertaining departure from the monotony of parenting, his sleep-deprived mother accompanies him out the door and across the street to the house where a party is indeed in full swing.

Guests with painted faces and elaborate costumes heartily welcome the mother-son duo, luring them in with the promise of free babysitting and loads of tasty treats.

But no one mentions the presence of a magician in their midst, a magician who knows how to make little children disappear.

1

———

e are sitting by the living room window overlooking our front lawn, reading *Room On The Broom* by Julia Donaldson and Axel Scheffler, when we see the first guest arrive for the party across the street.

Of course, we don't know for certain there is a party. No invitation was extended to us.

But why else would anyone turn up at another's door at one in the morning wearing a hat with a single tall feather sticking out and a purple cape that looks as if it would make the perfect tent for little Dorian because it is ginormous and lined liberally with tassels and pompoms and has little pinpricks of light, and whether they are night stars or glow worms or spangles, it is difficult to tell?

Although the one big reason it will not make a suitable tent is that it is swallowing the very ground it is trailing on, leaving behind a blackness that looks like it can be anything or nothing at all.

I sneak a quick glance at Dorian. He too is watching. With

5

the intense curiosity that only three-year-olds can muster. Also with non-judgemental awareness.

His face is impossible to read. There is no fear there. He doesn't yet know of all the impossibilities of life and the laws of physics.

It is as if when I popped him out, he left behind in my womb his entire quota of fear for several lifetimes, and I have been lugging around all the anxiety for both of us ever since, all while trying to not let it contort my face into anything other than intense curiosity (to mask the single-minded alertness) or non-judgemental awareness (to hide the paralyzing panic).

The child watches me more closely than any God has ever done so far.

The first guest climbs up the steps leading to the front door of the house across the street. Bright crimson in daylight, the door is now a rectangular hole darker than the surrounding night.

We don't know who lives in that house. We don't even know that anyone lives there. I have never seen any signs of life in that house. No unexpected twitching of curtains. No windows left open on warm, sunny days. No glow of lights from within when darkness falls.

But, it now strikes me, although I cannot see it presently, its front lawn is always neatly striped. No signs of neglect there. Perhaps the handiwork of an invisible landscape contractor. Or of gnomes.

The door opens to reveal a dim glow of light surrounding the silhouette of the first guest. He steps in, and the door shuts behind him. A sudden bright flash of light erupts from within the house, like a firework set off in silence, and momentarily paints all the windows Halloween-yellow.

Like in a cartoon, three things happen all at once. The roof lifts a little, the windows and the door pop out, and the walls billow like curtains in the wind.

And then a fourth thing. An orange-grey plume of smoke unfurls out of the chimney like a dragon's breath.

I blink, and the house goes dark and still once more. From what I can make out, all the parts of the house have sprung back into place.

"Who was that, Mumma?" Dorian asks.

I let out a breath I only just realize I've been holding. "Hmmm … I am not sure, sweetie. Who do you think it is?" A question for a question. Stalling tactic. I need time to make sense of it all so I can find the right words to explain without terrifying Dorian. He is not afraid. At least, not in any way that *I* can see. Plus this could be a useful exercise in imagination for him.

"Fiffer-Feffer-Feff," he offers.

My mind's eye conjures up the harmless image of the four-fluffy-feathered funny creature from the book, *Dr. Seuss's ABC*, and, as I toss my head back, an unexpected laughter leaps out of my throat and gambols away on the ether taking some of my disquiet with it.

"Yes, that hat." I acknowledge Dorian's brilliance without resort to excessive, or any, praise.

"Let's go see," Dorian says.

"See what?"

"Not what. Whom," he corrects me. "Fiffer-Feffer-Feff."

"But," I say, and nothing more. Because … but what? What am I going to say? That it was not really a Fiffer-Feffer-Feff that just sauntered into the invisibly dark house across the street? That I was only being patronizing when I applauded Dorian's observation? That we don't go about wandering the streets at one in the morning? Kill the spirit of curiosity before it has even begun to bloom? Finally, I have it. A way out. "We don't know who lives there, sweetie," I say.

"Why?" he asks.

Why? How does one even begin to answer such a question? Truthfully, I think.

"Well, we have not tried to find out, so we don't know," I answer.

Dorian thinks for a moment. An image of serene thoughtfulness.

"We can go find out now?" he offers. "OK? OK. OK."

That's Dorian. He will ask a question and also give it a favourable answer. *OK? OK. OK.*

He runs to the closet in the entrance hallway and drags out his jacket and boots and mine too. There is no talking him out of this one. Besides, what are my options here? Read *Room On The Broom* twenty or so times before he finally falls asleep? Or head out to what might be a festive occasion, a cause for celebration, filled with adult conversations and, for once, indulge in drinks and food prepared by someone other than me?

"OK. OK." I jump up with enthusiasm, but am unable to muster enough to match his.

2

$\mathcal{I}$ help Dorian wear his spring jacket and rain boots, and then run upstairs to change out of yesterday's clothes, stained with spices and finger-paint and coffee.

I opt for a summer dress, a pale yellow affair with a pattern of white lilacs stitched all around the hem. It is funny but I don't remember owning this dress, let alone having ever worn it. It fits me just fine. Whatever.

I sneak a quick glance at the mirror to make sure my hair doesn't look entirely like a bird's nest and my face doesn't look like it simply cannot belong to a human body.

Mission failed. Mirrors suck. They show you the truth without presenting any context, any justification, for it.

Mirror, mirror on the wall,

if you're gonna tell me that my looks appall,

then you better know better than to lie,

when I ask you, do you goddamn know why?

Jeez! Even my three-year old knows 'why', not 'what', is the most important question of all. Sure, he'll first lure me in by asking 'what', but it is the subsequent 'why' that gets him to the truth all the time. And so, remember this: what you see in the mirror is a fraction of the truth, the least important fraction.

"Mummum!" Dorian's voice cuts through my thoughts.

"Coming, sweetie."

I strap on my watch. It is half past one. If a fairy Godmother were to appear in front of me now, never mind the time, I'd ask her to endow a lifetime of restful sleep on me and Dorian, because I really want to sleep. I need to. And so does he.

That is what we both should be doing instead of getting dressed up to knock on the door of a neighbour we have seen not even once since we moved to this suburban neighbourhood more than a year ago.

This entire business, so out of routine, is something I don't want to get involved in, but then I think of the example I'd be setting for Dorian if I were to walk away from this now. My darling Dorian, all dressed up, waiting so patiently for me by the door.

"Mummum?"

"Coming, my precious."

I grab a shawl to wrap around my shoulders, a purchase from another lifetime, a red and maroon and orange affair, the colours of autumn blending in one length of velvety fabric with tiny silvery threads that shimmer with motion. Feet in boots, shawl around shoulders, Dorian's hand in mine, we slip out into the night.

$$3$$

Again, three things happen all at once.

Now the door is in front of us, and then it is gone.

Now the silence of the night is all around us, and then there is music, the rhythmic beats blasting out of the house into the very earth we stand upon, thudding into our hearts.

Now there is no one, and then a bunch of faces appear in front of us, all gorgeously painted in colours I thought only Dorian could concoct by pouring out all his paints on the floor and slip-sliding on them in that singular way that is solely his.

The designs are exquisite. Thought-provoking and comment-worthy. Blue-green whorls and swirls of peacock feathers, black and white spirals you cannot stare at without your head spinning a little, a burgundy sun with green quivering rays like a patient Venus Flytrap.

"Red triangles." Dorian points out, and I see another face painted in concentric triangles, starting from the nose in the centre, in countless shades of red.

A bright red gives way to scarlet and persimmon, flame red merges with vermillion and coral-red, which bleeds into carmine and crimson and cardinal, which merges with rust and burgundy and rosewood and maroon. Like a red triangular sun. Aflame at the centre, giving in to its own darkness pressing all around.

"Good job!" Triangle-Face grins at Dorian, squatting down to peer closer at him, her smile somehow seeming to form yet another triangle. Inverted, though.

"Look, the triangles are moving!" Dorian points a small finger at her, his eyes and mouth like three rings of surprise, as if he too is forming a triangle in response.

"What a clever boy you are!" Triangle-Face is delighted at having found such a keen admirer of her design. "The Devil is always in the details. But don't stare too hard or he'll pop right out and gobble you down!"

Dorian titters. Nervously, I think.

"I'm just kidding!" Triangle-Face pats his cheek. "You clearly know your shapes and colours though. Surely you deserve a treat for getting that right. Would you like some cake?"

Triangle-Face is definitely not a parent or at least not a well-informed one. We are not big on rewards and praises at home. It is all about helping develop a child's inner drive and motivation. Read your Alfie Kohn, babe, I want to admonish her.

And then, as I will find out later, I make my first mistake of the night.

I look at Dorian. His face is lit up. So I keep my mouth shut. Which is why he happily steps towards Triangle-Face and away from me.

Triangle-Face is ecstatic. She scoops him into her arms and sets him on her hips. "Say bye to Mumma," she says, her voice irritatingly high-pitched and childish, and I want Dorian to squirm and whine away from her and back to me. Stranger danger, child? Have I not taught you anything?

"Bye, Mumma," he shouts loud and clear over the sound of the music. "We're going to get some cake."

"What a delightful child he is!" Triangle-Face grins at me. "Is he allergic to anything?"

I am surprised she knows to ask. I mutely shake my head. And off they go.

4

"He'll be fine," a voice drifts into my ear as a hand gently holds my elbow and Venus Flytrap nudges me into this house in which the light is loud, bright and dark colours drift in and out of a smoky haze, and the music shakes the air within.

The tune is familiar, something I've heard on the car radio too many times to forget, paying too little heed to remember.

"What song is this?" I ask, as we press through a crowd of standing, swaying, moving bodies like branches of a tree casually probing the boughs of its neighbours.

I am not interested in the answer. Not really. I just need to shrug off this emptiness that has replaced Dorian by my side, even in the midst of this crowd, and pretend I am not too worried about him. I don't want to reveal all of this to Venus Flytrap.

The trouble is you never know what might prompt someone to call Social Services on you. You worry too much, you are a clingy parent. You worry too little, you don't care enough to be a good parent. Being a parent is like fighting a losing battle. The only trouble is you can quit fighting only once; that is only when you die.

Anyway, I see Dorian seated beside Triangle-Face at a long table filled with delectable sweetmeats, savouries, and a colourful assortment of cut fruits. That is where we head.

"Starboy," Venus Flytrap says, as she pulls out a chair for me right next to Dorian. He has already heaped his plate with slices of watermelon, mangoes, and oranges beside a thick slice of Black Forest gâteau. He knows the importance of colours in every meal. He now digs into his cake with intent.

I turn to Venus Flytrap absentmindedly. "What?" I ask her, the sight of my child safe and happy, and my proximity to him, stripping me of all the concerns I had nary a moment ago.

"Pardon?" Dorian butts in.

Venus Flytrap smiles and tousles his hair. "The song," she turns to me and says. "You were asking about the song. It is Starboy by The Weeknd."

"The Weekend?"

"Yes," she replies, "but no 'e' before 'n'."

"I want to be Starboy," Dorian declares.

"Sure." I shrug.

"What does starboy mean?" he asks. The 'what' question comes first. I am clueless but I make an attempt.

"I suppose it means a boy who shines like a star." I put my arms up and wiggle them and bring them down in a slow, wide arc, like a cheerleader without the pompoms.

"Why does the boy shine like a star?" That follow-up 'why' question. Entirely expected.

"Maybe if we listened to the song, we might find out everything about the starboy," I suggest.

And that is the second mistake I make that night in that spangled room where disco lights prick the air to the rhythm of the music, and grown-ups with painted faces dance on the floor beside the long table where Dorian and I are feasting.

5

———

"*A* starboy is someone who is super cool," says a man sliding into the empty chair to my right.

"Fiffer-Feffer-Feff," Dorian shouts.

But the man hardly looks like that beloved creature. The feather on his head is taller than Dorian is. The man (creature?) wiggles his eyebrows, which seems to make his feather sway and dance, much to Dorian's delight.

I look over my shoulder and there it is, that sparkling, earth-swallowing cloak, a piece of night sky for a tail.

"You have a wild imagination, young man," he grins. "But I am actually The Piper." He pulls a flute from somewhere within his cloak and offers it to Dorian. The child promptly puts it into his mouth and blows it like a whistle. The sound is mellifluous but not loud enough to pierce The Weeknd's Starboy still blasting from invisible speakers.

I turn to The Piper. It is only when I look at him closely that I realize I had been expecting the face of a cartoon. A bulbous nose and a wide mouth set in a face that should have stretched like elastic. Or something like that.

But no. Here is a man whose face is a study in geometry. All sharp angles and smooth planes, sparkling like a polished gemstone in the glimmer of the disco lights, as if he has swallowed the sun and the light is now shimmering through the pores of his skin. Clearly, I have been reading too many vampire stories on my Kindle during sleepless nights.

"Starboy is a great nickname for Dorian then," I say, using conversation to distract myself from staring at The Piper.

"Yes," he affirms, "although it is also a synonym for Casanova."

I promptly wonder if I should discourage Dorian from nicknaming himself Starboy. But I have also learnt that as far as Dorian is concerned, the forbidden fruit must be tasted, and the forbidden act must be carried out.

"Would you like to see a magic trick?" The Piper asks Dorian.

The child spoons some cake into his mouth and nods.

The Piper springs up from his chair and comes around me, then grabs one end of his glittering cloak and throws it over Dorian. I jump up but The Piper lays a heavy hand on my shoulder and keeps me glued to my seat, as he pulls back his cloak to reveal an empty space where Dorian was a moment ago.

"What the f—?" I begin but The Piper lays a finger on his lips and winks at me. If his gesture is meant to assuage me, it has the opposite effect.

I reach out to grab his cloak but he is swifter than I am. He swishes his cloak over the chair once again and drags it back to reveal Dorian back in his place on the chair, staring up at something.

"Whoa!" The child blinks at us. I grab Dorian and hug him, both relieved and embarrassed, as he squirms out of my grip to face The Piper.

"How do you feel?" I ask Dorian, as casually as I can in the face of what has just transpired. He has the nose of a hound when it comes to smelling desperation and fear. I give him a quick visual once-over. He appears unharmed, both physically and emotionally.

"Happy," he says.

"What did you see?" I ask, injecting some excitement into the question.

"Moon," Dorian says, his eyes glancing at the ceiling as if to coax whatever he had seen under the cloak back into existence. "Stars. Millions of stars. Billions of stars." He then turns to The Piper and asks, "How did you do that?"

"It's a secret." The Piper puts a finger to his lips. "Never tell anyone I keep a piece of night sky hidden in my cloak."

Dorian nods at The Piper in solemn understanding. "Yes," he says, and turns towards his plate. Unfinished business to attend to.

My breath is short and rapid, and my heart is still thudding for a way out of my chest, but it all appears to have been a harmless trick, at least as far as Dorian is concerned. Every moment of anxiety pertaining to him leaves me a little more permanently damaged than before.

The Piper bends over to me and smiles. "My apologies," he says. "I should have warned you."

"Yes, you should have." I am miffed. I also hate it when people apologize for their mistakes before I've had the opportunity to let my anger at their behaviour run its course.

"My apologies again." He bows and extends his hand. "Please allow me to make it up to you with a dance," he offers.

The absurd timing of his proposal makes me groan inwardly. No way do I want to dance with a man who just made my three-year-old child disappear from right under my nose. In fact, I should be running out of this party place and back to our home right now. That is the sensible thing to do, isn't it?

I glance at Dorian, as if a shoulder angel hovers over him, bearing the answers to all the important questions of this Universe. He is attempting to squish a pulp of mango into The Piper's flute. I do not bother to dissuade him. The Piper deserves this for the torment he has caused me. But would it not be in poor taste to thwart his attempt at an apology, no matter how ludicrous?

Triangle-Face and Venus Flytrap are locked in deep conversation on the other side of Dorian but they throw occasional glances at him. Assured they are keeping an eye on my child, I take off my shawl and drape it gently around his shoulders. Something of mine for him to hold on to in my absence.

And then I make the third mistake of the evening as I slip my hand into The Piper's and let him lead me away from the table, away from Dorian, into a slow dance, one hand held snugly in his, another on his shoulder, his arm draped around my waist and resting on the small of my back, firm yet gentle, Starboy having given way to a slow, lilting melody in which the music is not interrupted by lyrics. My skin starts to tingle as if some of The Piper's luminescence is permeating me.

"So, are you a starboy?" I ask him. I am still mad at him for making Dorian vanish.

He throws his head back and laughs. "It doesn't matter, does it?"

"You being a starboy?"

"Whether I am one or not?"

I smile and shake my head. I turn to look at Dorian, who is playing a game with Venus Flytrap. He points at her nose with his index finger just an inch away from her face, and promptly pulls it back as she springs her trap shut. He is quick, that child, and also a good sport.

"He seems to be a great kid," The Piper says.

"Oh, he's an absolute delight," I declare, still watching Dorian laugh as I sway in The Piper's arms.

"It must be hard, caring for a child," he says, with an unexpected softness on his face.

This is where conversations on parenting get tricky. To admit something is hard is almost akin to wishing you didn't have to do it. And yes, there are days I wish I weren't a mother.

But to admit it is hard without acknowledging it is beautiful too is like speaking a half-truth. Like a mirror presenting a fact without context.

And yet, to deny it is arduous is unthinkable. It is the kind of lie that can pull the rug from under unsuspecting feet, break hopeful hearts, banish faith, and instil fear in the minds of countless others like me.

Whether it is the shock of seeing Dorian disappear or the fact that no one has really commiserated with me until now for the difficulties of parenting, I say what I've never said to anyone else.

"It is. It is very hard. And many days I just want to give up. I wish for nap-times to never end. I wish for the morning to never come, just so that I can remain buried under the sheets. And yet, on other days, I think that all the magic of this Universe has manifested itself in the form of this precious child."

"No parent truly deserves their child, you know," The Piper sighs.

I turn back to him. "What do you mean?" I ask, although I can guess. If we believe we should not suffer the way we do for our children, then we also cannot lay claim to the unexpected marvels that come with watching a life bloom. I suppose that is what God must have felt during the creation of this Universe.

"Children come into this world, whole and pure, sacred and divine," The Piper explains. "Unfortunately, they are born to adults who are broken, who have strayed from their true selves. Surely, no adult has the means to preserve the sanctity of a child."

"That may very well be," I empathize. "But everybody was once a child. And who better than a child to remind us of that?"

The Piper narrows his eyes and asks, "Does that make you bitter? Remembering that you too were once as joyful, as uninhibited, but no longer are?"

I scoff. "On the contrary, I am delighted to have found my way back to what really matters, to who really matters."

I am beginning to feel a little annoyed with his judgements. True, the desires of an adult and the needs of a child remain in near constant conflict. But isn't that the crux of parenting? Finding a way to handle the duality of it all? Isn't that the essence of life?

The Piper smirks. "It can't be that simple. Sure, he's a

delight at this age, but you do know what they say about those teenage years, right? That is when most parents fail their children. Spectacularly."

I pull my hands away and step back from The Piper. "Are you a parent?" I ask him.

"I fund an orphanage," he says. "But no, I don't look after the children myself."

"That is a noble thing to do," I say because what I really find noble is his admission that he completely lacks parenting skills and has no basis, whatsoever, to judge the parenting choices that real parents like me have to make every day, every moment. But, of course, he does not get that.

"Yeah, I ended up with a bunch of kids and no grown-ups on my street. I was barely an adult myself back then. So I put them up in this empty house and hired a few hands to cook and clean."

"What happened to their parents?"

"Nothing happened to them," he wiggles his fingers in the air to form quotation marks around his utterance of the word 'happened'. "They were just the type of people who didn't deserve their children," he shrugs, as if helplessly.

A tiny terror forms a lump in my throat. "What do you mean?" I croak.

"They were cheats who didn't keep their word," he shakes his head ruefully. "No child deserves to grow up with such parents."

Something stirs in the back of my mind. A piper and his pipe. Children gone missing. Parents who didn't keep their word. I gasp. "Are you The Pied Piper of Hamelin?" I shout.

"The one and only," he smiles, and for the first time that evening I see how ugly and menacing a smile can be.

His razor-sharp looks are like a thousand blades piercing my skin. An unknown fear grips my body and I push past the dancing bodies and run towards the table faster than my mind can conjure up the thought fully.

But I am too late.

Dorian is gone.

6

In that house across the street from mine, where guests with painted faces feasted and danced to the rhythm of light and music only a moment ago, is now a silence, emptier but heavier than the darkness that has settled everywhere. That house is now like a hole in space and time.

A match is struck.

A candle is lit and placed on the table, now bereft of all the delicacies that had lured Dorian in like a moth to a flame.

Three fake faces glow in the candlelight, monstrous shadows flicker on the walls behind.

"Where is Dorian?" I scream and hurl myself at Triangle-Face, who is nearest to me.

I don't even reach her before the trio jumps up. Hands grab me and pin me to a chair. A rope is produced and used to bind me securely, even as I flail and kick around. The struggle is futile. The three settle back into their seats and watch me squirm.

"What have you done with him?" I yell. Hot tears run down my cheeks and neck.

"Nothing yet," The Piper says, twiddling with his pipe. "It all depends on you."

"What do you mean?" I snarl.

"You made three mistakes this evening," he says. "And that has cost you dearly."

"What mistakes?" I look around at all three of them but Venus Flytrap and Triangle-Face sit with no voice in their throats and no emotion on their painted faces.

"First," The Piper explains, sticking out the index finger on his right hand, "you permitted your child to partake of food offered by a stranger. Second," he sticks out his middle finger, "you allowed him to listen to songs completely inappropriate for anyone his age. And third, you simply left him with strangers just so you could seduce another stranger."

I nearly gag at his final accusation. He waggles his counting fingers at me with the kind of ill-placed delight a despotic principal would find in caning the palms of errant students.

I rack my brains for some acerbic retort, some witty comeback, but am choked with the absurdity of it all.

Sure, accuse me of bringing a sleepless Dorian to a never-before-seen neighbour's home at one in the morning only to stumble into a party filled with food and people and music.

But if accepting a man's request to dance because *he* wants to apologize is tantamount to me seducing him, then one of us is entirely in the wrong Universe at the wrong time in history.

I look at the trio, The Piper pacing up and down, Venus Flytrap and Triangle-Face sitting still as stones, all watching me, waiting for the next words to spill out of my mouth, mentally spinning the next web of lies and deceit to trap me in.

They are the only ones in this room now, the only ones who know where Dorian is, and that is all that matters, I tell myself. Not their judgements, not their insinuations.

I want to scream and shout and rant about how crazy they are and how unfair their accusations are.

But if there is one thing I've learnt in the past three years of looking after Dorian and fending off well-intentioned advice from unexpected quarters, it is this: it is almost impossible to argue someone out of their staunch beliefs.

And so I say, employing the calm and empathetic tone I have learnt to use because of Dorian, my darling Dorian, "I am sorry. I trusted you all even though, as you say," I nod towards The Piper, "you are only strangers to me. I trusted you the way I trust that Starbucks will not poison the banana bread I order for Dorian. I left him with you two," I look at Triangle-Face and Venus Flytrap, "and stepped not more than six feet away because he seemed comfortable with you. As for the song, I don't even know the lyrics to judge whether it is age-appropriate or not."

The Piper snorts, then slams a palm on the table. His theatrics have the desired effect of terrifying me.

"*Ignorantia neminem excusat,*" he says, pointing a finger at me. I don't need to ask him what it means. Ignorance is no excuse.

My undergrad professor of Corporate Ethics used to repeat a similar phrase so often it is quite literally the only thing I remember from the course I took in what must have been another lifetime.

Ignorantia legis neminem excusat. Ignorance of the law is no excuse.

The ridiculousness of it all makes me want to laugh. These three hypocrites here, not one with the balls to bring up a child. And I, bound to this chair, as if I were on trial for the neglect and abuse of my own.

"Where is my child?" I muster the courage to ask. "Clearly you are as concerned for him as I am. He must be terrified, wherever he is."

The Piper narrows his eyes. "*Ignorantia sit beatitudo,*" he says. Ignorance is bliss.

But who is ignorant, I wonder? Is he saying I am better off not knowing where Dorian is? Or that Dorian, wherever he may be, is completely oblivious to the goings-on here?

More tears spill from my eyes and I am unable to put up a façade of calmness anymore.

"I'll do anything to get him back, please," I whimper. "We all make mistakes. I'll be more careful henceforth. I promise."

The Piper looks at Venus Flytrap and Triangle-Face, who nod back at him. "You must answer a question then," he declares.

"Of course," I reply, sensing a glimmer of hope. Truth or dare? Seriously? Anyway, there is nothing so abominable in my past that I can't reveal it to bring back Dorian. "Ask me anything, please," I say, blinking back tears.

"You will have only one opportunity to answer." The Piper waggles his index finger again at me. "So think carefully before you speak."

"Sure." I nod fervently. Game on.

"Which of the three of us has Dorian?" The Piper asks.

My heart stops for one long instant.

"Which ... one ... of ... the ... three ... of ... us ... has ... Dorian?" The Piper repeats his question, spacing out the words for emphasis, and smirks.

The several implications of this question dawn upon me all at once.

The Piper has just admitted that one of the three of them has Dorian. There is no indication yet as to the state Dorian is in but considering how fanatic this self-righteous trio is when it comes to childcare, I assume that, at the very least, Dorian is physically unharmed.

Of course, he will not escape the trauma of this episode for the rest of his life but he'll have me by his side through all the nightmares and panic attacks that lie in wait for us. But right now, relief floods through me and I feel light enough to fly, were it not for the rope binding me to the chair.

And then the improbability of answering this question hits me like deadweight on my head.

Think, I command my brain.

Whodunnit?

Think!

I frantically bring up my memories of this bizarre evening thus far and search for clues. It is all a jumble. The painted faces, the strobing lights, the pulsing music, the dancers and the feast. Now that everything else has disappeared, it is hard to believe they were even here in the first place.

I look around. There is nothing but darkness punctuated by the flickering shadows of this ghastly trio dancing on the wall behind, even as two of them sit motionless like mountains and one continues to pace up and down, twirling his flute in his hand, as if immobility were anathema to him.

The flute! Hadn't he passed it on to Dorian before the dance?

I peer at it. There is nothing much to see. It appears clean. No mango pulp sticking out from one end.

When and how did The Piper retrieve it? He was dancing with me the entire time. Unless, maybe it wasn't him?

It could just as easily have been either of the other two, or the two of them in unison. But what were The Piper's words, the second time he posed his question?

Which one of the three of us has Dorian? I clearly remember he waggled a finger at me when he said 'one' for emphasis.

Or am I simply making a collage of memories in my head and force-fitting snippets of recollections into a path to lead me to a logical answer, when this whole situation is entirely bereft of sense and sanity?

I look at Venus Flytrap and remember the game of trap Dorian was playing with her. That was the last time I saw him. The realization makes me sick. I just want to get him back and get the hell out of here with him.

I might as well be taking a test and attempting to pen a thousand-word essay with only two minutes to spare, entirely aware of the futility of it all yet desperate to notch up my word count as much as possible.

But I also remember how good Dorian was at evading the trap.

No. It could not have been Venus Flytrap.

I remember from a *National Geographic Kids* magazine Dorian and I were browsing through in the library the other day that this carnivorous plant only traps insects and arachnids. Obviously, Dorian is neither.

I turn to Triangle-Face and stare into her eyes, seeking a clue, but I'm unable to look at her for longer than a few moments without feeling dizzy. It is as if I am endlessly falling into an optical illusion even though I remain exactly where I was several moments ago. Tied and bound to a chair in the house across the street from mine.

Triangle-Face was the one who had led Dorian straight to the table of goodies. Did she slip something into his Black Forest cake? A drug to make him drowsy, perhaps? Something to knock him out so they could quietly and swiftly slip him away in those few moments when I dared to look away?

These thoughts twirl endlessly in my mind until every new thought that springs up is no longer new, but very old and worn-out because of being repeatedly twisted and turned over in my head.

My throat is parched. My breath is swift and shallow. I feel an intense need for physical movement to stop this churning in my head.

I am staring too hard into the lines of thoughts zinging through my brain like a school of fish darting incessantly in all directions.

Don't stare too hard. Step back and reassess, I tell myself.

That's when it hits me.

Don't stare too hard.

Isn't that what Triangle-Face had remarked to Dorian at the door when he had observed her moving triangles?

The Devil is in the details. He'll pop right out and gobble you down!

Triangles. Devil.

The Devil's Triangle!

A lesson in geography from a very long time ago. What

was it called? The Bermuda Triangle. That's it. Where everything disappears, without any explanation.

But what if I am wrong?

I am terrified. I look at the three of them once more.

The Piper.

Venus Flytrap.

Triangle-Face.

If I had to choose one of them to look after Dorian, whom would I trust the most?

The Piper shows no remorse for luring children away from their parents.

Venus Flytrap was more inclined to talk about the music than about the anxiety that was pounding through my chest as Dorian was being led away from me within moments of our stepping into this dastardly house.

Triangle-Face did try to terrify my child with her talk of the Devil but promptly admitted it was a joke. Was that a warning?

Don't stare too hard.

What would Dorian have done? Of course, he would have tried to stare harder than was humanly possible. That was no warning from her. It was an invitation. Harmless on the face of it, but enough to entice any inquisitive child.

"Triangle-Face!" I shout before I can think anymore and invalidate my most recent hypotheses.

Time skids to a halt. The Piper freezes mid-stride. Venus Flytrap pauses mid-breath. Only Triangle-Face exhales, as though letting go of a breath held for far too long.

But before she can utter a word, The Piper hurls his cloak over all of us.

I instinctively close my eyes. A darkness smothers me. I hear a shuffling. And then, a soft cry.

"Mumma!" A shout right into my ears.

Dorian! So close! But I can't see a thing.

I flail my arms and legs to free myself from the ropes, but I'm strangely swathed in what feels like fabric.

I open my eyes. The night sky has fallen on my face. I push it away and try to hold it up. Silver stars shimmer in it, tinier than pinpricks.

Only, as my eyes adjust to the darkness, I see it is no longer black. Strips of red and maroon and orange merge and un-merge above me. What first looked like stars are no longer star-shaped. They look like tiny filaments. Confetti left over from a party.

I claw at this thing, whatever it is—it feels like fabric—and pull it away from me.

An avalanche of light blinds my eyes, and it takes me a few moments to realize it is the sunlight pouring from the east-facing window of Dorian's bedroom.

I whip my head around, and there is his three-year-old face, peering into mine with inquisitive eyes. My heart is pounding, but I try to stay calm and not alarm him.

"Wake up, Mumma," he says. "It's morning."

"Are you alright? How are you feeling?" I ask him, gently dragging him into a hug and hoping he will not discern the insane pace at which my heart is racing and inquire about it.

What I really want to do is squeeze him into a tight embrace, give him a hug so tight that he becomes tiny again, a foetus I can carry forever in my uterus without fear of losing him to unhinged strangers in this mad, mad world.

"Yes, I am OK," he says. "Are you alright?" Always the copycat.

"Of course, I am, sweetie," I say, wondering what he remembers of the previous night and how I can coax it out of him without sending the alarm bells ringing, which would be sure to shut him up.

"Did you sleep well?" I ask, pulling back to scrutinize him surreptitiously. He looks just fine. Bright-eyed and alert, as if he's had a good night's sleep.

He nods, then pouts. "But you didn't finish reading the book."

"Which one?"

"*Room On The Broom.*" He jumps up and reaches for the book, which now lies by the side of his floor-bed. "Read it now," he says, thrusting it into my hands. Surely, the child is unharmed?

I need to know what he remembers, and so I ask, "Oh, why did we not finish reading it last night, honey?"

"Because we had a party," he says. "Now read it."

"Did we now?" Dread pools in the pit of my stomach but I only display an acceptable moderate level of interest on my face.

"Yes. Read it, please."

"Where was the party?"

"In the kitchen. Now, read the book, Mumma." I hear the beginning of a whine.

I am almost tempted to threaten him that I will not read the book unless he tells me everything he can remember. Is he traumatized by everything that happened? And where the hell had that crazy trio hidden him when they were torturing me? So I change tack.

"Did we have cake at the party?"

He nods. "Black Forest," he volunteers. "It is my favourite."

"Who gave you cake?"

"You gave me," he says. "Now read it, please."

Dorian inherits his stubbornness from me. I want the answers to all my questions as badly as he wants me to read the book. And his responses seem to suggest he has a recollection of an entirely different party altogether. One that I am sure did not take place. I push as far as I can.

"Did anyone else come to our party?" I ask.

"No, Mumma," he is exasperated now. "It was just you, me, and the cake. Now read the book ple-ee-ee-ease."

I wonder if the three crazy creatures we encountered last evening have somehow altered Dorian's memory so that all he remembers about the incident are only the good bits of it, and not the horrifying parts. I make one last attempt.

"Was Fiffer-Feffer-Feff at the party?" I ask.

Dorian thinks, silently.

"Like in that book, Dr. Seuss's ABC?" I add.

Dorian shakes his head. "I don't know," he says.

There, I have lost him. *I don't know* is sometimes the child's equivalent of *I don't want to talk about it*. I have pushed too far. Or perhaps, he sincerely does not know. Either way, I have no recourse now but to drop the conversation and read *Room On The Broom*.

7

We come down to make breakfast after having read the book four times.

First, I head into the living room and look out of the window to see if the house across the street from ours is still standing or, like Dorian's recollection of last night's adventures, has changed into something else entirely. A swimming pool. A tennis court. Or a restaurant, perhaps?

Nope. No such luck.

It is still there.

The front lawn is still tame, refusing to grow wild. The crimson door remains closed, as if it is not a real door but merely an image of one painted on the wall.

Nothing twitches. Nothing explodes. Nothing seems amiss.

I wonder if I can ever sit by the window and look out without recalling the horrors of the night. Not even half a day has gone by since I lost my child, albeit temporarily, and found him again by some uncanny stroke of luck.

Was it really Triangle-Face who had hidden him? And if so, where?

Does Dorian really not remember anything as it all happened?

Or does he remember only the bits he wants to? The bits that matter to him? Like the joy of a party? Cake?

Or is this some sort of merciful act by the trio? Did they only want to scare the bejesus out of me but ensure my child was not harmed in any way?

Perhaps, the past is nothing but all the stories we tell ourselves. About ourselves. About others. About everything that has transpired.

Maybe I should stop harping on about how I lost Dorian, almost forever, and instead think about how I got him back. Whether it was by a stroke of pure luck or indeed some strategic thinking on my part, I will never know.

Somewhat troubled, somewhat relieved, I turn away from the living room window and head into the kitchen, where Dorian has already climbed on to the countertop, awaiting his breakfast.

I pour some readymade pancake mix into a bowl and add water to form the batter. It occurs to me I ought to serve him something healthier, like eggs and fruits, in the mornings. Tomorrow is another day, I tell myself and sigh.

"Mumma," Dorian's voice chirps up. "Shall we ask Alexa to play songs?"

"Sure!" I am thrilled my child can find ways to keep himself entertained when I am otherwise occupied.

"Alexa," he calls out.

The rim of the cylindrical gadget lights up in a dancing blue that runs along the perimeter a few times.

Satisfied that he has Alexa's full attention, my three-year-old commands, "Alexa, play Starboy by The Weeknd."

A SUITABLE COLOUR FOR A GHOST

A SUITABLE COLOUR FOR A GHOST

Storytime is my realm. I am the expert at spinning bedtime stories for my four-year-old child. It's a ritual both of us look forward to every evening, much to my husband's consternation.

Tonight, I intend to tell my little one a ghost story. Not to spook him, but as an exercise in imagination. A blurring of lines between fact and fiction.

Little do I know that he has a ghost story of his own to share with me. A tale that is truer than all the ~~lies~~ stories I've been telling him all along.

1

———

Sometimes only my four-year-old appreciates the kind of stories I make up.

(Truth be told, he is only a few weeks shy of this fifth birthday. He is too old to be called a four-year-old, but I will never call him an almost-five-year-old. The process of aging is so utterly irreversible I do not wish to hasten it at all.)

I digress.

(I tend to do that a lot. Consider yourself sufficiently warned.)

Anyhoo, as I was telling you, sometimes it is only my four-year-old who totally gets the kind of stories I concoct and relates to them the way every writer desperately hopes every reader of their work would.

This evening, I've made up a story about a green ghost, inspired by something on those lines I had read in my teens. Must have been one of those mysteries featuring either Nancy Drew or The Three Investigators or The Hardy Boys.

My bet is on Nancy Drew. No real reason for that choice. Just a hunch. Or a long-ago memory. That's all. More likely a jumble of several long-ago memories and perhaps I've gotten them all wrong.

A quick search on Google will surely solve this mystery. Better still, ask ChatGPT!

But it will also reveal other nasty truths including that Carolyn Keene, the purported author of the Nancy Drew series, is not a real person. It is not the name of a real person but an alias used by several ghostwriters who wrote various Nancy Drew stories over the years.

There! Did this revelation take *you* by surprise? I cried when I first found out. So, let's leave the algorithms out of this mystery for once.

I tend to digress a lot. I did warn you about that. But what else can I do? I suddenly find myself in possession of so much time I don't quite know what to do with all of it.

So, I make up stories. A lot of them. Not lies. But stories, as in fiction. The kind people like you are willing to read and listen to, simply because I've confessed upfront these are merely the workings of my imagination.

I can tell you the damnedest things that would make your heart stop beating, but you'd coax it back into rhythm by reminding yourself that everything I've said so far is make-believe.

We all have our coping mechanisms. I digress and reveal more than I ought to. You deny and tuck away as fiction all the truths I serve you on a silver platter.

Whatever!

Whatever works for me, whatever works for you, everything is acceptable. Well, almost everything.

Back to the green ghost. In one of those teen sleuth stories, a green ghost flits through walls.

(Spoiler alert! It is later explained that the villain uses phosphorous, which reacts with oxygen to emit a green glow effect.

This scientific explanation will come in handy should my four-year-old get too spooked. Anything that can be explained tends to evoke less fear.)

In my story, a green ghost flits in and out of the walls of our home, as if looking for something. And in the end, I will reveal it is no ghost but a green alien who has somehow crash-landed in our backyard and needs help to return to its home, a green planet containing mostly phosphorous in its atmosphere.

(This part of the story is completely inspired by the Paw Patrol episode *Pups Save a Space Alien*. And if you do not know what Paw Patrol is, please ask the first four-year-old you come across. They will gladly supply you with all the details you'd need and more. Besides, whatever you may think, my tendency to digress is not entirely out of control.)

I can barely wait for bedtime to arrive tonight, so excited I am about my latest story.

Ever since a freak accident, six months ago, rendered me physically incapable of picking up books and reading to my little one at bedtime, we've had to find alternatives.

We've slipped into the habit of making up our own tales, although I do feel a twinge of guilt that this exercise in imagination, no matter how thrilling, comes at the expense of reading time. Ah, well! We can't have it all.

I sit patiently in my little one's room, making not the slightest noise, and keep my lips pursed lest the story should tumble out of my eager mouth well before bedtime.

My husband is in his element this evening, cooking and

bantering with the little one. He must have had a good day at work. Or an absolutely terrible one.

The creamy aroma of mushroom pasta and the peals of laughter of the father-son duo waft up the stairs. I sigh, knowing dinnertime would take way too long this evening.

I must have fallen asleep as I was waiting, for I wake up with a start, roused by the sound of laughter, too close for comfort, as father and son boisterously dash up the stairs and ready the tub for a bath.

Eventually, they tumble into the little one's room, giggling and squealing. The sound of my child's laughter stirs my soul more than any piece of music has been able to in my lifetime.

"Hi, Mumma," the little one waves to me. I smile back.

My husband doesn't even cast a glance my way. I don't blame him. It is important to know the difference between what a person *will* not do and *can* not do. It helps put almost everything in the right perspective, one that helps everyone move on.

While he dresses our child, I try to think of the various ways our story for the night could take on a life of its own and wander down unexpected paths. I simply can not wait to discover the little one's take on the overall plot.

The fresh scent of bath soap mingles with the mild fragrance of baby lotion. I inhale deeply to keep my impatience in check.

All dressed, my child jumps into bed, pulls the covers to his chin and declares, "Mumma will tell me stories tonight."

My husband frowns. "Again?"

"Yes."

"You haven't read books in a long time," my husband contends.

"Of course, I have," my little one says. "I read at school all the time."

My husband pinches the bridge of his nose, a telltale sign he is exhausted and about to relent, knowing better than to prolong a debate with our four-year-old at the tail end of an excruciatingly long day.

"OK," he gives in.

My little one squeals with delight. "I love you, Dada," he says. An expression of genuine gratitude.

"But close your eyes and fall sleep early, alright? I don't want you staying up too late, talking to yourself."

"I don't talk to myself," the little one protests. "Mumma is here with me."

My husband looks around the room. Grief tugs the corners of his lips down into a deep frown. I freeze. He doesn't even look at me.

Finally he gives up, kisses our child on the forehead and then leaves the room, turning the lights off on his way out. Light from the landing spills into the room, eliminating the need for a special night lamp.

Story time at long last!

"I've got a terrific story for you today," I say.

"Me too," my four-year-old says, turning towards me.

"Cool! You go first."

"It's not really a story. Because it is something that really happened. I narrated it to Dada but he didn't believe it."

"I'm sorry it turned out that way. But hey, if you say it really happened, I believe it did."

The little one nods, as if he had known all along what I'd say.

"So, what was it that you told him?" I ask.

"The other night, I woke up in the middle of my sleep and saw a green light lying right next to me."

If I'd had a heart, it would have skipped a beat. But I don't, so I simply stay mum and wait for him to fill the silence with words.

"It was on my right side," he continues. "So, I turned around and slept on my left side."

"I wonder what that light was."

"Maybe light from a car outside?"

Under normal circumstances, that would have been the most plausible explanation. "That could have been it," I say. "What did you feel when you saw the green light?"

He thinks for a moment, then replies, "Nothing. I was just sleepy, and the light was too bright. I turned away and fell asleep again."

A child who is not easily spooked by weird lights and glowing objects in the dark is a rare breed indeed. Still, after what I've just heard, I can't bring myself to share with him my story of the green ghost. Not tonight.

Instead, I make up a silly tale of a man who looks all over his house for a pair of spectacles that sit perched atop his head the entire time.

That's the beauty of being with a child. Life becomes novel all over again.

I stay until he falls asleep. And then a little longer. I watch the slow rise and fall of his chest with every breath and marvel at how his long eyelashes kiss the tops of his cheeks.

And for the first time in six months, I don't fall asleep beside him. I flit out of the window and perch myself on a branch of the sunburst honey locust tree outside our home that provides me with an unobstructed view of my sleeping child through the window.

It is rather noisy in the tree. Restless ghosts of folks who grew up or lived in the area hang around to keep a protective eye on the families they've left behind.

I prefer noise to loneliness tonight, and so I stay in the tree and mull over suitable alternatives for green, the all too standard colour designated to ghosts and phantoms and apparitions. Even glow-in-the-dark stickers are often an eerie green. Nothing like the psychedelic green of new leaves in spring or the deep green of trees in summer.

One of the more talkative ghosts asks me what my child's favourite colour is.

My little one always says his favourite colour is rainbow. He won't choose only one.

It makes me glad. Because that way lies endless possibilities.

MEMORY GAMES

MEMORY GAMES

On the morning after his seventh birthday, Skyla gives her son a gift without his knowledge. Also, without his consent. She gets all his painful memories excised from his brain.

She considers it the best gift of all. The memory of a perfect childhood.

But no one could possibly gift something that simply does not exist. At least, not without unfortunate consequences.

Memory Games secured an Honourable Mention in the L. Ron Hubbard Writers of the Future Contest (July—September 2023).

1

Skyla's heart leapt into her throat as the technician gently lifted Rowen's head with gloved hands and draped what appeared like a black swim cap over it. Thin black wires emerged from the base of the cap and fed into a machine, no bigger than a shoe box, placed on a low side-table beside the bed.

A skull-and-crossbones image on the contraption would have been apt, Skyla thought, chewing on her fingernails nervously.

"Are you certain this will work?" she asked for the umpteenth time that morning. It was all she could think of.

The technician smiled and nodded without looking up from her work, which at this point entailed tugging the skullcap evenly from all sides and ensuring it covered the child's head completely.

"No side effects?"

"None at all," the technician replied, again without looking up.

Skyla chewed her fingernails and tried to calm herself

down. Other than the fact that she knew what was about to happen, there was nothing in this room that appeared threatening to her or her seven-year-old boy in any way whatsoever.

Rowen lay fast asleep in a soft bed with a white sheet and pillow covers with a printed design of blue waves and colourful little sailboats all over. A duvet with a matching cover was pulled up to his chin. Even in this anaesthetic stupor, he slept with his mouth innocently open and his favourite Squishmallow, Rutabaga the caterpillar, tucked under the duvet beside him.

The bed was up against a pastel blue wall on which fluffy white clouds and V-shaped gulls had been painted. A piece of sky in the basement.

Skyla caught an occasional whiff of fresh laundry, a breezy, light-hearted scent, but she couldn't tell if it was her imagination reacting to the sight of the wall décor or the effect of a subtle fragrance dispenser tucked out of sight.

The theme of blue skies and white clouds continued on all the walls. Against one wall beside the bed was a neat arrangement of shelves in white and pastel shades, bearing books and an assortment of toys. Against another was a large white table and bright yellow swivel chair set up under a board to which were pinned what appeared to be family photographs with children laughing, grown-ups beaming, sun shining, and grass gleaming.

It all made the room appear as if it had sprung into existence straight from an IKEA catalogue. Fresh and charming. Exactly what a child's room was supposed to look like.

They were in one of the basement rooms of what had

turned out to be a very well looked after Georgian house. Skyla had lured her newly seven-year-old to the place citing the necessity of annual medical check-ups.

"Why aren't we going to Dr. Kamal then? We always go there," Rowen had asked, much to Skyla's chagrin. Her boy was growing up too fast. He knew too much. He remembered too much.

She made some excuse about Dr. Kamal being away on vacation and that had seemed to satisfy Rowen, who promptly ran into the gardens of the house to inspect the rows of tulips that were in full bloom.

She would have to erase his memory of this conversation too; she couldn't afford to have him inquiring Dr. Kamal about a vacation that had never taken place.

A path through the garden had led them around to the back of the house where a steep flight of stairs and then a bright red door with a mischievous-looking brass pixie on the knocker granted them access to the room they were now in.

Skyla had been pleasantly surprised at how pleasing and welcoming the room was, while Rowen had delightedly run straight to the shelves of books and toys. She had never managed to achieve that effect in Rowen's own bedroom back at home, so it gave her some consolation that the procedure was set to be conducted in a room like this, although a pang of grief plucked at her heart that her child would leave this place holding no memory of it.

A large screen took up the entire wall opposite the bed. It flickered into life as the technician, now having discarded her gloves, pressed a button on a flat handheld device smaller than her palm, pointing it at the screen.

The technician was a short, plump woman with silver hair

that sprung up in thick but obedient curls around her kind face. Curious brown eyes peered from behind tortoiseshell glasses with chains. She was smartly dressed in a pastel pink skirt suit but she smelt of muffins and icing, of cookies and chocolate.

Skyla decided to call her Mrs. M in her mind. A codename. Like in the James Bond stories. There was a decidedly furtive air to it all. Besides, M could also stand for Memories. That made it easier to remember.

Moreover, Mrs. M had declined to reveal her name nor had she asked Skyla for her or her child's names. The less they knew about each other, the less likely they'd compromise each other, Mrs. M had insisted, especially since the procedure was only in its nascence.

"You won't believe the number of times people swear they can weather the risks and side-effects, but the instant trouble comes knocking on their door, they come looking for me to blame," Mrs. M had explained to Skyla on her first visit about a month ago.

Yet, the technician had insisted that there would be no side effects to what they were about to attempt. Skyla felt the need to verify again, now that the moment of reckoning had arrived what with Rowen lying with that contraption on his head at one end of the room and on the other end, fractal images curling and unfurling, expanding and shrinking in an eerie psychedelic dance on the screen.

"But you said there won't be any side effects?" Skyla asked, narrowing her eyes. "Then why would people come looking to blame you?"

The old lady looked up at Skyla with understanding eyes. "It is terrifying to face up to what you've desired for so long, isn't it? Because what if it doesn't solve the problems you had hoped it would?"

Tears moistened Skyla's eyes and she let them spill. Mrs. M held out a box of tissues from which Skyla pulled out one and dabbed at her eyes.

"It is," she sniffled. "What if it messes up his mind in some unexpected way?"

Mrs. M waited for a few moments before replying, "It's quite like forgetting. He won't remember what he doesn't know he once knew." She paused, as if allowing Skyla to untangle and correctly interpret that particular sequence of words. "You cannot miss what you don't know you had."

That, Skyla understood very well.

2
______

Fatherless since the age of three, Skyla had grown up with her mother and grandparents. Life had been just perfect until three years later she had stumbled upon a photograph of her father carrying Skyla in one arm, his other arm wrapped around his wife, the three of them laughing into the camera at some joke the photographer had said, wide, open-hearted grins lighting up their faces. That photograph in all its sepia-tone glory had caused her world to burst open in a way she had never known before. She began to remember things it was impossible to remember.

She could see clearly in her mind's eye how he stayed up all night holding her when she refused to sleep in her cot, how he'd throw her high up in the air and catch her every single time, laughing and giggling, how he could spend an entire afternoon pushing her on the swing without complaint, how he made eating all her veggies one of the most delightful parts of mealtime.

But those memories brought along with them the raw,

heart-rending grief of what she'd never have again: life experiences with her father.

Ever since, being fatherless became a significant part of her identity, her only identity, and her excuse for getting into trouble and sabotaging her own life and future, until John had come along and whisked her off her feet. Then he too went and died before Rowen was born, and if that wasn't a sign from the Universe, what else could be?

She had to see to it that Rowen did not suffer the same fate she had. She couldn't let him become a victim of his own memories.

3

———

When the tears stopped and Skyla found she could speak once more without hiccuping for breath, she nodded and said, "OK, let's do this."

Mrs. M taught her how to work the remote. Right arrow for fast-forward. Left arrow for rewind. A play/pause button in the centre. And a red round button at the bottom for delete.

The system would not prompt for a confirmation, Mrs. M warned. The instant Skyla pressed the Delete button, the memory would begin to get erased until she pressed the button again.

"And there is no way to retrieve any of the deleted memories?" Skyla asked.

Mrs. M opened her mouth as if to say something, then peered at Skyla through her tortoiseshell glasses on which the reflections of the fractal images on the screen danced. It was almost cartoon-like and Skyla was gripped with a sudden urge to laugh at the wild absurdity of it all.

"There is a reason you want those memories gone, isn't it?" Mrs. M said at last.

Skyla simply nodded, keeping her lips pursed, afraid of what strange sound might spill out of her mouth if she let it. A strangled laugh. A cry of uncertainty. A sob. A scream, perhaps?

"Then let's get on with it, shall we?" Mrs. M said. She went up to the desk and chair beside the screen and rolled the yellow swivel chair towards Skyla, gesturing to her to sit on it.

"You will be at it for a few hours," Mrs. M said mysteriously as Skyla sank into the soft chair, holding the remote gingerly in her hand, afraid she'd press the wrong button accidentally.

"Good luck," Mrs. M said, then left the room, closing the door quietly behind her.

Skyla pulled herself closer to the bed and looked at Rowen for a few moments. Why hadn't anyone ever told her how hard life could be?

Her mother and grandparents had always insisted that given time and trust, she'd be able to face any situation and overcome any challenge that life threw her way. For a while she had believed that, but then she lost John and found out that there were always exceptions to the rule.

The sight of Rowen's sleeping face steeled her resolve. Now this was a difficult task she'd see through, she told herself and set to work.

4

——————

A heart beats inside a womb. Liquid darkness flows all around it. Voices in the distance, from somewhere outside.

A tiny fist reaches out, touches the wall.

Squeals of delight sound on the other side. Something glows. Someone calls out in a voice so loving and tender.

What lies outside? The infant wants to know. He is eager to slip out and see. He can't help it. He has to push his way through, head first.

The screams are deafening. Muffled still, but louder than ever before. He can hear the startling pain in those wails. Is something wrong?

Push, push, he hears someone say, and he feels the walls of his home pushing against his feet, squeezing him further and further through the birth canal.

And then he is out.

A shock of cold hits him all over, and now it is his turn to open his mouth and draw breath and let out a cry.

That seems to please everyone. There are tears and

laughter, and now he is being placed on something soft and warm, on someone safe, someone who loves him so much, he can already tell. Someone who wraps his arms around him and coos into his ears and kisses him all over and makes him feel warm and safe all over again.

5

———

Skyla hit the pause button. She needed a moment, just a moment.

This was ridiculous. Even though Mrs. M had explained to her exactly what it is she'd see on the screen, she hadn't expected it to be like this. She hadn't been prepared to see the past unfold from her child's mind. Not from the instant he had come into existence inside her womb.

Did people really have memories of that time? How is it that you could spend an entire lifetime designating each moment to memory, to history, only to have very little recollection of any of it afterwards? Where did all those memories disappear to?

But they didn't really disappear, did they? Rowen's memories were right here, being extracted from some unknown part of his brain by that skull-cap on his head and fed into the shoebox machine on the other side of the bed from where they were projected onto the screen like a movie.

A video recording of childhood, except it was all from Rowen's perspective. And she could feel everything he had felt at that point in time. All his fears and his joys, his curiosity about this new world he had found himself in, and his frustration at not being able to make sense of it all right away.

It was as though she had become him, in reliving his memories and feeling all his feelings.

The initial shock wore off and Skyla continued her journey through Rowen's memories, more intrigued and less intimidated now.

There were many, many happy memories, many more than she had believed. Good! There'd be less to wipe out, she thought and that gave her some relief.

Every time she saw her smiling face through Rowen's eyes as she bent down to pick him up for a cuddle, pride surged through her heart. She had been a good mom, she really had tried very hard.

There she was, the first person he saw when he opened his eyes after a daytime nap.

There she was again, squatting, arms outstretched, face lit with a wide smile, as he went down a little slide and slid off and straight into her waiting arms.

There she was again, cleaning a bruise on his knee, putting a bandaid on it and kissing it, promising him it would heal in a jiffy. There had been a time when her assurances were all he needed to bounce back from pain and disappointment, when her word had been enough to restore him to a place of safety.

And then her first mistake.

At the age of two.

Skyla could feel Rowen's terror grip her entire body as she saw her own face bearing down on her on the screen, red with anger, her mouth spitting harsh words at her toddler who had somehow managed to topple a large basket full of thermocol balls on to the floor and had been jumping up and down happily, chasing those slippery balls, scooping them in his little hands and throwing them up, calling out, "Se-no, Se-no," able to manage only a childlike warped pronunciation of 'snow'.

Rowen's fear and shame flooded her entire body as he sat, in his memory, in a corner, tears streaming down his cheeks and snot filling his nose, little hands clamped over his ears, watching his mother hoover up all the little balls that had given him so much delight now disappear into that loud, roaring machine, which was still no match for how loud and angry his mother's bellows were as she continued to curse his very existence and his innate ability to make a mess around him wherever he went.

6

Skyla hit the pause button again, and only when the video on the screen froze and the sound was cut off, did she hear the whimpers that wracked her body alternating with her own loud, uncontrollable wails filling the room.

She whipped her head around, worried the commotion may have awoken Rowen. He remained asleep, completely oblivious to the goings-on around him. His face glowed in the light from the paused video on the screen in that pale, ghostly way that skin shines under moonlight.

Was he dreaming? Or was he safe in the depths of some dreamless sleep, a realm of the subconscious she had long lost access to ever since John had died and Rowen was born and her mind had once again opened up to the terrifying inevitabilities of loss and grief, of pain and sorrow?

Skyla looked back at the screen where her own angry face from five years ago glared down at her, eyes grown too large to be held back in their sockets anymore, teeth bared and lips curled in a snarl as her mouth was frozen in mid-expletive, a face twisted and contorted in anger.

And for the first time she could reach out and touch the fear that hovered just beneath her skin. And when she touched it, she could go even further and feel the pain and grief lurking beneath it all.

In that moment, as Skyla sat in a yellow swivel chair in the basement of a beautiful Georgian house, trusting the contraptions set up by an unknown Mrs. M to weed out memories of bad experiences from her child's mind and psyche, she saw her world expand.

The spirit that throbbed deep inside her being swelled and ballooned and grew larger and larger, a bubble widening beyond the walls of this room, past the boundaries of this house, breaking every visible and invisible barrier that stood between her and the rest of the world.

And in doing so, her spirit encompassed the hurt and the pain of every child that had ever been birthed and brought into existence in this world, and throbbed with the grief of every mother and father that had ever had to struggle with the impossible responsibility of raising a child well.

In the inexplicable vastness of her heart she could now hold the pain of every form of life that had once been a helpless infant or a vulnerable seedling, that had ever been wronged, and alongside she could also hold deep compassion for everyone that had caused pain, knowingly or unknowingly, monsters not even of their own making.

Because, Skyla was finally beginning to see that her pain was no different than that of the world, the way she hurt her child and the way she was hurting inside were just as valid as the terror and fear the little one felt in his veins, just as valid and honest and true as the confusion she herself must have felt when at the receiving end of rebuke and reprimand, no matter how well-intentioned, from her own mother or her grandparents, even from her teachers or that random stranger on the road who likely believed he knew much more about raising a child than every other parent on earth put together.

And if that were true, then no sin in this world was unpardonable because if no one was of their own making alone, but a product of every external influence and life experience that had begun shaping them even before they were born, that was shaping them even now, then no person's sin, or even virtue, was of their own making.

Something released itself from deep within Skyla's gut, something like an absolutely rigid knot of guilt that had weighed down her soul to inaccessible depths came bubbling up from her belly to her throat and slipped out with the sigh that escaped from her lips. Whatever it was, drifted away, like the white tufty clouds that dotted the blue sky imagery on the walls around her.

She forced herself to look into the angry face that scowled at her from the screen. "It's OK," she whispered to her red raging face on the screen. Her past-self from five years ago continued to stare at her disbelievingly, for it could never be OK that she had ever inflicted such torment on her child, could it?

"It's OK," Skyla whispered again, "you're only human. Besides, we're fixing it now, aren't we?"

Perhaps it was her imagination, or perhaps it was her change in perspective, but the image on the screen began to soften. The anger in that frozen face seemed to dissolve and Skyla could clearly see the grief and fear that lurked beneath it all.

The grief of losing John. The fear of raising a child as a

single mother. The worry of not being able to do him justice. The constant, nagging fear that she was always falling short. The harsh critical voice inside her mind that insisted she had already screwed up Rowen's life in every which way possible.

Because didn't all the parenting experts insist that every behavioural problem you exhibited now, every fear and anxiety that held you back, had their roots in your early upbringing?

The first seven years of our lives were all that mattered, and then we spend the rest of our lives undoing what was done to us in those first seven years. Who had said that? Was it Steiner? Or was it Montessori?

Whoever it was, their words were now being regurgitated by every parenting expert, and goodness, how many of them had proliferated in this world in just the past decade?

It was as if everywhere she turned, someone stood with a book or a podcast or a video or a word of advice, intent on showing her just how badly she was screwing up every single moment as a parent, as a mother, as a human being.

She too was not a mother of her own making. She too was heavily under the influence of all these external stimuli, whether she resisted or succumbed to them, it didn't matter. She was under their influence all the same, and it shaped and twisted her in ways she could barely ever control.

"It's OK," she whispered to Skyla-on-the-screen again.

Then she rewound the video to the instant where her angry tirade had begun, and pressed the Delete button.

7

Rowen was seventeen years old when a girl first broke his heart.

"What did I do wrong?" he kept asking his mother over and over again, and when she had no satisfactory answers to give him, he disappeared into the music of Pink Floyd and Metallica that poured through his headphones into his ears, drowning out all voices from outside and from inside his own head.

Skyla pottered about in Rowen's room on days like these. Gone were the nightlights shaped like a star and a crescent moon. Gone were the growth mindset posters she had put up on the walls for encouragement and motivation. Gone were the baskets full of LEGO bricks and pieces that had, at one point in time, taken up a permanent spot besides Rowen's bed.

The walls were now covered in posters featuring the album covers of Pink Floyd and other bands the names of which weren't familiar. A large triangle splitting a single beam of light into a rainbow of colours. Another featuring a quartet wearing more metal than clothes, glaring out of the poster with kohl-lined eyes in a way that could have been threatening or enticing, it was always hard to tell.

The table and chair had grown larger with Rowen, as had the bed, but they had also grown tidier over the years. Gone was the scent of baby shampoo; the room now had an unusually thick scent of deodorant mingled with sweat.

Skyla threw the curtains and windows open. She had always loved the fact that Rowen's room had large windows on both the southern and western sides. Light from the late afternoon sun flooded into the room, riding on a cool, gentle breeze carrying birdsong and the perfume of spring nascence.

Rowen didn't seem to mind her presence and occasionally stepped out of his heartbroken stupor to join in her attempts at tidying up. For that, she was grateful.

She had heard horror stories of how teenagers hated having their parents in their space. Ever since Rowen was a toddler, she had been dreading that eventuality, and even when it never came she couldn't help worry that some day it would happen and her carefully constructed life would collapse without warning all around her.

"It hurts so much, you know," Rowen said, watching leaf-shadow dance on the wall behind his bed. "I never knew anything could hurt so much."

Skyla could have told him then, recounted all the times she had hurt him with a sharp rebuke or a nasty glare. She could have told him about all the times she had hurt him, sometimes even relishing in the sense of power and control it used to give her, and his surprising ability to bounce back and forgive her and love her unconditionally as if nothing untoward had transpired in the first place.

But those memories were gone for him, etched stronger in

her mind though, and after his seventh birthday she had been nothing but the perfect Zen mother.

Understanding when he had glued his T-shirts together. Unflappable when he had come home from the playground with a bloody nose. Calm when she had been called to the emergency room where the school had had to send him when he had ended with a broken ankle after a rather energetic game of basketball.

Serene and tranquil as she was now, watching him nurse a broken heart, even as her own heart cried inside at the sight of her son's pain.

"This is the most difficult phase," she said, quelling the urge to convince him that this too shall pass, that other girls will waltz in and out of his life for no fault of his, and that life will continue to throw curveballs his way. He was a strong man now, she wanted to remind him, not burdened by any childhood trauma that would trip him up in life. She had ensured that at least.

He nodded, then resumed listening to the music he had paused to engage in that brief snippet of conversation. His hair fell over his eyes and he pushed it away. He had never liked that, any barrier between him and the world and all that it had to offer, not even when he was a child.

8

———

Rowen's psychiatrist looked uncannily like Mrs. M, if Mrs. M hadn't aged a day in the past seventeen years. It was a sign, Skyla thought.

Only, the psychiatrist called herself Dr. Rodriguez but that didn't change the fact that she was a short, plump woman with a curly silver bob and brown eyes framed in tortoiseshell glasses. She was dressed in a dark skirt suit, like a senior executive of a Fortune 500 company, but her perfume had the impossible aroma of chocolate and cookies.

Her office wasn't decked out like a child's bedroom but was all dark wood furniture with plush sofas and cozy bookshelves against a backdrop of forest green walls. Pot lights lit up the room in a warm, comfortable glow.

At Skyla's insistence, Rowen had started seeing Dr. Rodriguez a few months ago, shortly after he had turned twenty-four. After that first heartbreak seven years earlier, Skyla saw her boy grow addicted to getting high on weed, drop out of university and backpack around the world, and fall in and out of love faster than day could turn into night and back into day. It was almost as if he had developed an aversion to everything that was good and stable and secure in life.

A few sessions in, Dr. Rodriguez had wanted to meet Rowen along with Skyla, if she was willing and able, to better understand his childhood. Skyla had been terrified at first when her son had texted her about his psychiatrist's request, but she had promptly replied "Yes" with conviction.

It must be Mrs. M, Skyla thought, sitting across the desk from the kind, old lady. Why else would the psychiatrist want to meet her? Rowen was an adult now, old enough to attend therapy on his own without a parent accompanying him.

"Have we met before?" Skyla ventured, worried that Dr. Rodriguez would deny knowing her.

But the psychiatrist smiled kindly and said, "Perhaps our paths crossed a long time ago. I've been in this line of work for a very long time now."

Hope bloomed in Skyla's heart. Perhaps she could confide in the psychiatrist, tell her the truth, after all.

She turned to look at Rowen who had made himself comfortable on a wide two-seater sofa in the centre of the room. Legs in socks dangling over one arm of the sofa, he lay supine, taking up the entire length. He had one arm over his forehead, another over his belly. He appeared relaxed in a way Skyla hadn't seen him in a long, long time.

"Does he confide in you? About what ails him?" Skyla asked, turning back to face Dr. Rodriguez.

"Rowen is looking for the perfect woman," Dr. Rodriguez said, looking at Rowen in a manner of contemplation. "He seeks a perfect relationship, and I daresay you are to blame for that."

Skyla shrank back at those words in a frisson of anger. Unfazed, Dr. Rodriguez turned to look at her and smiled. "I don't mean that in an accusatory way. I'm sure you know we all recreate in our adult life the patterns we experienced in childhood, especially with our primary caregivers."

"I know," Skyla said, "which is why I strove to be a perfect mother to Rowen. Maybe I tried too hard, but his father died before he was even born, you know that? I took great care to ensure that home remained a safe and comforting place for Rowen. I wanted him to trust he could always count on me, that no matter what life threw at him, he always had a safety net in me, in home. Shouldn't that have made him a strong man? Capable of weathering all the ups and downs of life? That is what all the parenting experts said. Back then, at least!"

"I understand," Dr. Rodriguez said. "Rowen says he's had a very happy childhood, that he can't recall a single unpleasant experience with you. But, you see, sometimes it's what we don't know about ourselves that haunts us. The ghosts of our forgotten selves."

Skyla was shocked. "You know, don't you?" she gasped.

"Know what?"

"About his memories," Skyla whispered, afraid of what she'd hear next.

The doctor nodded. "I know he cannot access them, not his early ones anyway. We have tried hypnosis. It didn't work." She peered into Skyla's eyes, almost accusingly, and asked, "Are we looking for something that no longer exists?"

Skyla barely managed to croak out the words through the fear that seemed to be strangling her. "I thought it was for the best."

9

"Our brains do not develop fully until we are in our mid-to-late-twenties," Dr. Rodriguez said, as she slipped something like a black swim cap over the top of Rowen's head.

He was asleep on the couch, heavily sedated.

Dr. Rodriguez fetched a blanket, which Skyla draped over Rowen and tucked under his chin. An eerie sense of déjà vu filled her being.

"Are you saying what was done can be undone?" Skyla asked hopefully, without turning to look back at Dr. Rodriguez.

"We can always try," the doctor said.

Skyla spun around to face the doctor. "And what side-effects will it have this time?"

"I shall repeat what I said to you seventeen years ago, and I will also tell you something I've learnt since."

Skyla held her breath. This was as close a confirmation she'd ever get that Dr. Rodriguez and Mrs. M were one and the same person.

"It is true," the doctor was saying, "you cannot miss what you don't know you once had. But perfection is never a worthy objective to pursue. The more acceptance we have towards our mistakes and failures, the better off we'll be in the long run."

Dr. Rodriguez/Mrs. M/Fairy Godmother pressed a concealed button on the side of the sofa by Rowen's head. A white screen rolled down from a recess in the ceiling in front of a bookshelf-lined wall.

Clearly, Dr. Rodriguez/Mrs. M had kept up with the latest technology, and that instilled some confidence in Skyla, a sliver of hope that she could set things right, notwithstanding the doctor's advice to be more tolerant towards her deeds and misdeeds, she realized wryly.

The doctor pressed a remote in Skyla's hand. Right arrow for fast-forward. Left arrow for rewind. A play/pause button in the centre. And a green round button at the bottom for Retrieve.

The system would not prompt for a confirmation, the doctor warned. The instant Skyla pressed the Retrieve button, the memory would begin to be implanted back into Rowen's brain until she pressed the button again.

"I thought you said the memories were deleted forever," Skyla said.

"No," the doctor said, pressing her lips to hide a grin. "You asked me if there was no way to retrieve any of the deleted memories. And I didn't quite give you an answer."

10

———

"Lilly poured thermocol balls all over the kitchen the other day, you know?" Rowen said to Skyla one evening just as she was about to leave for home.

She had spent the entire day caring for her two-year-old granddaughter while Rowen, now thirty-one years old, attended medical school, training to become a brain surgeon, and Kiara, his wife of five years, ran a flourishing publishing business out of her downtown office.

One last month of summer, and then Lilly would begin to attend a popular daycare in the neighbourhood. Skyla's services as a daytime caregiver would no longer be required, except in the case of illnesses and emergencies.

"You've been a tremendous help," her daughter-in-law had said very graciously, "and we can never thank you enough for all that you've done. It would do Lilly some good to spend more time around children her age now. Lilly loves you. Rowen and I do too."

Skyla had understood, yet she couldn't help feel a little sad.

It was as though her nest was about to become empty once more.

"She loves thermocol balls, yes," she replied absent-mindedly to Rowen as she stepped out of his home into the bright summer evening.

The sky was a delicious blue. White tufty clouds drifted past like sailboats. A gentle breeze tousled the tops of the maples that arched over the quiet and pretty suburban street Rowen and his family lived on.

Skyla slipped her sunglasses over her eyes, then turned to him and said, "You did too, when you were her age, you know?"

"Really?" Rowen scratched his days-old beard. His eyes were bloodshot from lack of sleep. "I bet that drove you mad."

Skyla laughed. "Very!"

But the very next instant, tears sprung into her eyes and she was glad for the sunglasses that hid her grief from Rowen. "It was the first time I yelled at you."

Her voice faltered, and once the words started to come out, she couldn't stop them. "There was thermocol everywhere, and it was just the two of us, just me all alone, really, trying to look after you and worried that you didn't have a father in your life. A boy needs his father, you know? And I knew you'd be needing your snack and a nap real soon, but I hadn't slept well in days, and the sight of all those ... all those little weightless balls everywhere, it ... it just drove me mad, having to add yet another task to my endless to-do list. I am so sorry, Rowen, I am so sorry."

The tears streamed down her cheeks, and Rowen was startled. "It's alright, Mom. I don't even remember you ever screaming at me. But even if you did, I get it. I totally get it."

Rowen pulled Skyla into a hug and said, "Kiara and I would have hardly stayed sane had it not been for you doing the bulk of the work when it came to Lilly. And you had no one, Mom. You were awesome, Mom. You didn't have to be perfect. But you were just the perfect mother for me."

Skyla's heart sang with a gladness she hadn't felt since the day John died. "Thank you," she whispered, as she pulled away from Rowen and patted his cheek. A grown man's face.

She was not one of those mothers who still infantilized their adult children. Yet, she couldn't help but feel amazed at how her little boy had grown up to become such a kind and generous man, a father himself now, his heart so wide open it could now hold all the pain in this world and not crumble under all that weight.

She had been so terrified that Rowen would remember all the wrong things that she herself had forgotten all the wonderful memories of his childhood.

She knew what to do now. At their next family dinner, Skyla would bring out all of Rowen's childhood pictures and videos—and she had stocked up an almost endless supply—to regale her son and his family.

And to remind herself of the only truth that mattered, that no life was perfect but that she had ensured that the good times far outnumbered the bad ones.

"Thank you, Rowen," Skyla said, then wiped her tears and turned to walk the three blocks to her own apartment, the sun still generously spilling warm light on her head and the wind caressing her cheeks tenderly.

THE GOLDILOCKS ZONE

THE GOLDILOCKS ZONE

Newly suburban mother, Sonia, yearns for the support of a community to raise her almost three-year-old son, Aarash.

But she discovers, to her great disappointment, that her new neighbourhood is filled with far too many gestures of polite friendliness but no real friendship.

Until one day a bike accident transports them into a parallel world that promises her the perfect community she has been longing for.

But being part of a community means her child will no longer be only hers. Will she be willing to make such a sacrifice?

1

———

t doesn't take me long to get used to riding the bakfiets. The basket bike. Aarash is admirably patient while I take the bike for a spin in the vast and mostly empty parking lot behind the bike shop.

My test-ride lasts less than five minutes, for most of which the sound of a child's cries keeps ringing in my ears. I decide I can learn on the go and return to the shop, confident of getting the hang of riding the beast sooner than later.

Aarash is waiting happily by the entrance in a blue helmet with Thomas The Tank Engine, Percy, and James grinning from the top of his head.

"Look what I chose," he leaps up at the sight of me and points to his helmet.

"Thomas!" I squeal with equal excitement.

"And Percy and James," he adds.

"You look like you're all set to go on a bike ride."

Aarash's face falls. "Not now," he shrugs. "Maybe later."

"How was the ride?" Nikhil squeezes my hand.

"Was he okay?" I ask Nikhil.

"Yah! He was having fun. Tell me, how was the ride?"

"Great!" I say. "Another practice ride, and I should be good to ride with Aarash."

Aarash, our only child, has a name that means the first ray of the sun. He is thirty-four months old. Not yet three years old. No longer two-and-a-half.

2

_____

There is a series of moments I wait for every morning.

After we've had breakfast and Nikhil has left for work, Aarash climbs into the basket of the bakfiets, and we set out.

First, along Belvenia Road, past 4026, the home of Johann and Nataliya, our elderly Yugoslavian neighbours.

Then past 4050 Belvenia Road, where a tall ginger cat is perched inside the window, watching us with the kind of relaxed alertness that every human being in the world today aspires to achieve.

"I want to go there," Aarash once said, pointing to the cat.

"I know, sweetie, I would love to go meet that cat too." First, validate. Empathize. And then only reason. "But that is not our house. We can't just walk in there," I replied.

He thought for a moment, watching the cat with the kind of relaxed thoughtfulness that every grown-up desires to reclaim.

"Goldilocks!" he declared.

It took me a moment to first make the connection, and

then a second moment to marvel at the fact that my toddler had concocted such an incongruous link between a ginger cat and a fairy-tale heroine, and yet another moment to loudly laud his observation, and a final fourth moment to silently congratulate myself on this unexpected instance of motherly pride.

Up we continue now along Belvenia Road, past the bus stop in front of 4100, an apartment community for the elderly. I look for a familiar face in the row of first-floor balconies. An 86-year-old lady who walks her dog and always stops for a brief chat. I see her and we wave. I know her dog's name. Tanner. I don't know hers. I worry that when she dies, it will take me a very long time and a new tenant in her balcony to find out.

"I'd love a ride in that basket," another familiar voice hollers. It belongs to a plump, old lady with a jolly face who lives in one of the ground-floor apartments and is almost always in her tiny front yard, chatting with someone or the other. The very sight of her cheers me up.

"You can wait for your turn," Aarash reminds her. He's a real hoot.

And on we go and turn left onto the bike path, the Centennial Bikeway. And this is when I invariably tell myself I love Burlington. The city in Ontario, I mean. I have never set foot in its more popular namesake in Vermont. On the other side of the border.

We moved here a year ago from Toronto. From a one-bed condo in North York, to be more precise. A half-hour subway ride away from downtown Toronto.

When Hansal, an old friend of ours visited us from

London, UK (not to be confused with London, Ontario), he looked around and asked, "Have you ever played SimCity?"

Nikhil nodded, and I shook my head.

"Toronto looks like that," he explained. "A patchwork of random buildings built by amateur video game players. No character. No history. No vision." Well, obviously, it doesn't hold a candle to the UK.

But Burlington? I already love it here. What's not to love about a city where you are only a stone's throw away from the beach? Where it is legal to ride your bike on the sidewalk? What's not to love above a city that has a dedicated bike trail running through its heart and by the shoreline?

Don't move, my well-meaning friends in the city had warned us. "You," one of them had pointed a finger at me and said, "don't even have a license. You'll never survive in the burbs."

Look at me now. Suburban mom of one. Bike-rider. Eco-friendly. Making do with what I have.

The bike path winds past brambles and hedged backyards. An occasional rabbit skitters past. Robins and blackbirds swoop and soar. A tiny bridge leads us over a gentle stream, and we stop to watch a family of ducks, just sitting and doing nothing else at all.

We've had a very wet spring, so much so that the local beach has not yet opened for the season. But Burlington has been parched for a week now.

The sky is blue, the clouds are white, the sun is pleasantly warm. Lunch is packed and stowed under the seat alongside another bag carrying diapers, wipes and a change of clothes, and an entire day lies ahead of us for the taking, a day that seems to have spilled out of one of Enid Blyton's Famous Five books, brimming with adventure and fun.

"What is behind the sky?" Aarash asks.

I look up, my heart soaring at the kind of questions he conjures up while also sinking a little at the thought of the kind of answers I'll have to concoct. How does one even begin to attempt an answer to such a question?

"Maybe more sky?" I ask in return.

"Maybe," he nods, and relapses into silence.

I bought the bakfiets for the joy of conversation with my child sitting right in front of me rather than discarded and forgotten in a rear trailer, out of sight, out of mind.

Yet, our rides have transpired in silence more often than in conversation. The concoction of summer sun, the gentle bumpiness of the ride, and the buzz of katydids and cicadas often lull him to sleep.

We brake to a halt at the traffic lights at Cumberland Avenue. Just on the other side of the street, where the bike path resumes, is a steep, downhill slope that takes us down faster than any slide Aarash has been on.

And here it is. The moment we both wait for.

"Look what's coming up!" I holler, as the light turns green and I push forth, cranking the gears up and riding faster.

"Woohoo," I scream as the bike hurtles down the slope, preparing to splash through an unexpected puddle that Aarash spots at the bottom.

This is the moment I wait for each day.

The moment of free fall.

The moment in which I don't have to think about what to cook for our next meal or try to remember if it has been too long since the last diaper change.

The moment in which I don't worry about whether my little one will grow up and fall into prison or prostitution.

The moment when it ceases to matter that I've been unemployed for the last few years and we don't have enough money to go on vacation because the sun and the sky and the breeze of all of the world are right here, encapsulating my little one and me and our bike in an inexplicable bubble of happiness.

This is the moment in which I understand that parenting is all about wondering which will explode first: my head or my heart.

Turns out the answer is my head.

3

*L*ater, as I try to conjure up a memory of the crash, my first on the bakfiets, I will slot the events into a sequence that will reek of logic.

Aarash and I will talk about it over and over again, concoct a story from a memory, until he is reassured that an accident doesn't have to mean the end of our carefree rides down the bike path.

Right now, though, a number of things happen at once.

An abrupt flash of pink and grey.

A swerve and a thud.

A loud hiss and a meow.

A screech and a groaning scrape.

The ground turning sky blue. The sky turning concrete grey and grass green.

Aarash slip-sliding out of sight.

Terror paralyzing my throat and jaws.

No opportunity to scream.

Vision consumed by blackness.

4

———

"Wake up, Mumma, it's morning!"

Tiny lips press upon my cheek.

"Thank you, precious." I hug my child, keeping my eyes squeezed shut, hoping to cuddle with him for a few more minutes of sleep. Aarash has other plans.

"Look where we are!" He shakes my shoulders as something soft and cold and wet shifts swiftly under me.

I open my eyes and the first thing I see is Aarash's beautiful face stretched into a grin. Behind him is the vast sky and a warm, distant sun.

I sit up.

Under and all around us are sand and water and horizon as far as the eye can see. The water is cool and light. No smell of salt in the air. Lake Ontario, most likely. Has the Burlington beach been opened for the season?

A bunch of children splash about in the water near us. People I may or may not have seen before but can't quite place are sprawled on beach mats or loungers, reading books or doing nothing.

I look behind and find the bakfiets parked there, our lunch and diaper bag still miraculously stowed under the basket seat atop which now lies a pale pink Canadian Sphynx, curled in a Fibonacci spiral.

I know nothing about cats. It just so happens that our neighbour Cindy at 4020 Belvenia Road owns a dog and two cats, one of which is a Canadian Sphynx, nine months old. I wonder if the creature sprawled in our bakfiets is Cindy's.

"We're at the beach," Aarash jumps up. "Summer is here!"

He leaps into the waves and runs toward a group of three- and four-year-olds, frolicking in the water.

This is not Aarash, I think as I look at him. Aarash is quite like Nikhil, watchful, cautious at first in any new situation.

I am the one who throws caution to the wind, confident of figuring it out as we go. Okay, correction. I *was* the one who *used to throw* caution to the wind.

I am a different person now, the kind that feels anxious and worries that something is amiss at the sight of her usually reticent toddler playing with a bunch of unfamiliar peers on an unknown beach.

Thankfully, I know when not to complain. I can't remember the last time I was not needed by Aarash, and so I take this moment to watch my child lose himself in play. It is quite meditative.

Something velvety brushes against my arm from behind, and the naked, fur-free, velvety Sphynx makes her way to a spot beside me. She looks at me with eyes yellow like the distant sun.

I wonder if she is asking to be petted. Where I come from, that great land of myths and spirits on the other side of the world, I'd be deemed a grave sinner if even a single hair from the body of a cat were to fall to the ground on account of me. Even an offering in gold weighing more than the cat, now missing a strand of hair, made to Lord Shiva, the Great God of Destruction, would not relieve me of the burden of my sin for eternity. Or so I was warned in my younger days by grown-ups, well-intentioned no doubt.

I look up and see Aarash throwing occasional glances my way in the midst of his play with his newfound friends. That strange child, who watches me more closely than any God does. I must think of the examples I am setting for him. Besides, Canadian Sphynxes surely have no hair.

I reach out to stroke her under her chin but before I can, she transforms into my animal-loving, red-haired neighbour, Cindy, dressed in yoga pants and stretching into a graceful Marjaryasana, looking like a 60s celebrity.

"Surprise!" She grins at me.

"Cindy!" I yell, pulling back my hand. "Surprise, indeed! Though shock would have been a more apt word. What are you doing here?"

"Waiting for you, Sonia," Cindy replies, as she sits comfortably beside me. "And I've been waiting for a very long time. Most mothers end up here even before their first-borns turn one."

And just like that, I feel like an instant failure again, anxious that I have committed some irreversible mistakes on this parenting journey that will scar Aarash forever.

"Where are we?" I ask.

Cindy gets up. "Let's go for a walk," she says, and I follow.

I need to tell Aarash where I am headed but he is out of earshot, so I wave my hands to get his attention.

"He'll be fine," Cindy assures me, and a part of me wants to believe her but a bigger part of me won't allow it. Surprisingly, I quell my fear for once and walk.

"Let's not go too far then," I say. "What is this place anyway?"

"Welcome to the Goldilocks Zone!" Cindy announces.

"It sure looks like we are in the midst of a fairy tale," I chuckle.

Cindy looks a little alarmed. "You do know what a Goldilocks Zone is, don't you?"

"Hmm … not really," I admit. "I hope we won't run into any hungry bears though." Stop talking, I tell myself, before I reveal any more of my ignorance.

"A Goldilocks Zone is a place where everything is just right," Cindy explains. "It is usually used in the context of stars. It is the area around a star where it is neither too hot nor too cold, and the temperature is just right for liquid water to exist on any planet in that zone. And where water exists, so does life."

"Like on Earth," I say, eager as a student willing to learn and understand.

"Exactly. Now let's take that concept and apply it to our lives. Don't you wish your life conditions felt just right? Not too rushed yet not too slow? Not too much nor too little to do? Especially with a little child to look after?"

I want to let myself break apart right here and now and tell Cindy everything about what a delightful child Aarash is yet how hard it is to care for a little one.

How there are days when I look at the poetry that he is and realize that watching him play is the best form of meditation I have come across.

And yet there are days when time seems to have come to a

standstill, but somehow, I continue to fall into an endless abyss, and I think this is it, I will not survive this day to see the sun set and rise yet again.

But I don't. I don't tell Cindy any of this because I don't want her to call Social Services on me.

Now, I am not being paranoid. As a mom, the first thing I realized was that people are always watching and judging your every move, though very rarely in your favour. Wasn't it only last week that a nosy neighbour in Hamilton reported a mother for letting her three-year-old play in their fenced backyard, unsupervised?

So, I throw my head back and laugh instead. A hearty, confident laugh that I ardently hope will belie my absolute ineptitude at playing mom. "With a child, there's always too much to do and too little that gets done," I say. "Either everything's happening all at once or nothing is happening at all. But it doesn't feel wrong. You get what I mean? All the messiness. The sleeplessness. The inadequacy of it all. The ordinariness of it all. Isn't that what it's supposed to be?"

"That is what the world will have you believe, m'dear." Cindy is ecstatic, as if I have unwittingly steered the conversation in the direction she was aiming for. "The truth is … and bear in mind, this truth has been hidden from mothers, from women, for aeons. Motherhood doesn't have to be messy or inadequate or ordinary. You do not have to be sleep-deprived. The truth is, your child, he is not *your* burden alone to bear."

The truth always stings. I feel myself burning up from within, my stomach churning, my face growing hot, my nose and lungs refusing to help me breathe, even as the cool breeze whips my unwashed, but mercifully short, hair about my face.

The sun remains bleak in the distance, and the water cool beneath our feet.

I stop walking and look around to check on Aarash. My incredibly delightful child. Not even in my darkest hours have I deemed him a *burden*.

More children have joined the group he is with. Taller, bigger ones with surprisingly great observation skills yet very little awareness of the world immediately around them. They are roughhousing, and Aarash is standing on the fringes, watching, as he always does.

"He'll be fine," Cindy says and nudges me to continue walking.

But I don't feel fine. I feel anger and caution and anxiety all bubbling up from somewhere deep inside of me, a dormant volcano waking up, ready to jolt the world from its oblivion, its disregard.

"So, whose burden is he then?"

"Every child is the responsibility of the entire community," Cindy says. "You know the old adage … it takes a village. And that is what makes this place perfect. Just right. Everybody pitches in. You help care for a bunch of children when you can, and their mothers help look after Aarash. How much time do you get to yourself these days? An hour? Or two? Imagine what you can do with eight, ten hours of child-free time on your hand each day. All the poetry you can write, the stories you can read, the songs you can sing, the worlds you can change. All that without having to lose any sleep ever again."

5

_D_o you remember I told you about Hansal? That old friend of ours who visited us from London, UK (not to be confused with London, Ontario)? The one who likened Toronto to a SimCity development?

Aarash was not even a year old when Hansal visited us. I remember telling him I wish I had forty-eight hours in a day. Twenty-four to devote to the care of Aarash. And twenty-four to live the life I'd had before Aarash, and all the lives I'd have lived had he not turned up unexpectedly in my womb more than three years ago.

"It is a tough choice," Hansal had said back then. "An impossible choice."

Cindy makes a compelling argument. Which new mom wouldn't want more time, more child-free time to devote to matters that have nothing to do with her child or her home?

It makes sense now, what Cindy said earlier, about me being late, about other mothers turning up here in this picture-perfect, just-right Goldilocks Zone even before their infants turn one, willing to sacrifice the individualities of their children at the altar of community.

But I will not be fooled for an instant into believing that another person could ever love my child as her own.

Truth be told, I've never had much love for children in the first place. I love Aarash with as much ferocity as gentleness, but it is as if the intensity with which I feel for him has left me even more indifferent to his peers. I have certainly no contribution to make to this system of communal caregiving.

And I shudder to think of the consequences that Aarash may be made to face for my inability to coo over and care for another's child as my own.

"There must be a huge price to pay for such a gift?" I ask.

Cindy is silent for a moment but to her credit, she says, truthfully, (or so I think), "No mother has asked that question in over a hundred years now."

"Perhaps they were too tired to think," I say, letting the sarcasm creep into my voice.

"Yes." Cindy nods. "But to answer your question, there is indeed a price to pay. Not everyone considers it to be astronomical though."

"What is it?"

"Right now," Cindy begins, "all you can think of are all the things you could do if only you had a little more time, a little more sleep, a little more energy. Most of your thoughts are of all the lives you think you can have if only you had a little more help with Aarash. When you leave him in another's care for the first time, your head will swell with thoughts only of him. And everything else will cease to exist. All the stories and songs and poetry of this world will no longer be alluring in his absence."

"Why on earth …?" I open my mouth to protest the glaring preposterousness of her proposition, but Cindy holds her hand up and raises her eyebrows and I am stalled.

"It will take you a while to find meaning again in a life in which Aarash is not eternally present. How long? That depends entirely on you. Mothers who join us earlier take no longer than a week. Two, at most. You've waited far too long to join us. It will take you longer. It will be harder for you. But the more you delay, the more difficult it will be."

It doesn't take me long to see the dichotomy of it all. Even as I wonder if all the decisions I've made until now have led me and Aarash and Nikhil down a horribly wrong path, something tells me I need to trust myself a little more. I look at Aarash for an answer.

This gentle child, moving through this world at his own pace, unperturbed by all the noise and frenzy around him, already at home in this world where countless others are miserable and lost even after decades of existence. He stands out like the first ray of sunshine in the morning.

Who am I to tear him apart from his true self now only so that he can grow up to haunt the corners of this world like a lost soul, searching for the very home he was pushed out of as a child?

And for what? For more time for me? For more Aarash-free time? For more time for me to deny the existence of this child who is more exquisite than poetry, whose voice is the melody of this Universe, who is a completely unpredictable story unfurling right in front of my very eyes every day, every moment, and who has changed my world in ways I didn't even know was possible?

Whom I deem a blessing is a burden to another. What I

believe is a huge price to pay, the absence of my child, is another's idea of a gift, a rare privilege.

"And what about Aarash?" I keep coming back to the same question in every situation. What about Aarash?

"What about him?"

"How long will it take him to adjust to this new arrangement?"

"Look at him." Cindy shrugs. "He has already adapted."

The group of children has grown so large it is a darned crowd out there, and I struggle to find Aarash at first. But there he is, waist deep in water, jumping right into a big, frothy wave that crashes down upon him.

"Children can be quite resilient, if only we can trust them to be," Cindy says with finality.

Suddenly I feel an acute sense of absence, an Aarash-shaped hole that I know not what to fill with.

What if Cindy is right? What if it is too late? Who am I without Aarash? Who will I be when Aarash grows up and won't need me any longer?

But does that mean I should abandon him now when he still needs me?

True, he has been playing for the last half hour or so without calling out to me. An unexpected first for him. But how much of this development is because of being in the Goldilocks Zone and how much of it is age-appropriate behaviour?

And then it strikes me. Sure, Goldilocks found all the things that were just right for her. But what about the bears?

The story ends with three hungry bears, deprived of a homemade meal and left with a broken chair and ruffled beds to deal with. Someone always has to pay a price.

All along we've been deluding ourselves that it is the mothers who have been making the greatest sacrifices.

But the ones who truly suffer in all this charade are the children.

The infants, who are expected to sleep through the night so that their parents can sleep, undisturbed.

The toddlers, who are expected to keep themselves engaged so that their parents can take a cell phone break.

The pre-schoolers, who are expected to demonstrate emotional restraint, a feat that most grown-ups have rarely aspired to, let alone achieved.

All the children, who are resented for simply being children in a world of adults. They are the ones who pay the price.

I have a sudden desire to get away from Cindy, from this stupid place with all its illusion of everything being 'just right'. For that is what it is. An illusion.

Because wanting to have it all is akin to wanting to have nothing at all.

The desire for forty-eight hours in a day devalues the twenty-four that exist, ripe for the taking. In the absence of the four dozen hours I want, I spend the two dozen that I have moaning about the other two dozen that I don't have.

What a laugh!

When we want everything, we get nothing.

Everything becomes nothing.

All becomes none.

Voila! I have concocted my own koan, I muse.

The realization of this makes me suddenly giddy. I have a sudden urge to fly, my spirit is soaring, but my body is at first too heavy to be lifted into transcendence.

And then, I let go. I let go of all the ideas and notions of how everything should be and bask in the delicate impermanence of this moment in which Aarash and I exist, safe and happy.

I am flying now, over to Aarash. Cindy and her sermons are a distant memory. I am free at last, free from the opinions and judgements of others as well as from my own doubts and anxieties. Perhaps, this is what enlightenment is.

"Mumma," I hear Aarash call out to me, the sound of his voice lifting me like the wind I am sailing on.

"Coming, precious," I call out, as I glide towards him.

An arm shoots out from his vicinity and shoves him into the water. And just like that, Aarash disappears.

"Noooo!" I scream and swoop down on the murderous arm and snap it into two.

Shrieks and cries erupt as if there were three million, and not merely three dozen, people on the beach.

I duck underwater to look for Aarash.

And all I see is a black, bottomless pit.

All I hear is an angry roar.

And the last thing I recall is my own inner voice cursing me for not having signed up for swimming lessons yet again.

6

———

"**M**umma," Aarash's voice snaps me out of my reverie.

"What, cutie?" I ask. I am a little giddy as if I've travelled a great distance too fast and haven't yet had a chance to catch my breath.

"Green light," he says.

And here we are again. At the traffic lights at Cumberland Avenue. Across the street from where the bike path resumes, from that steep, downhill slope with the puddle through which we crashed into the Goldilocks Zone.

"Are you okay?" I ask Aarash, remembering him being held underwater by a child whose hand I had broken. "Who pushed you underwater?"

"When, Mumma?" Aarash asks.

"At the beach."

"You said the beach is still closed."

"Oh, right. It is, isn't it?"

When the light turns green again, I push forth reluctantly. We cross the street and are now at the top of the slope.

We've had a very wet spring and the lake has spilled over the narrow strip of beach where we spent most evenings last summer. It hasn't rained in over a week now. The beach remains closed but there is no puddle on the bike path.

"Woohoo," I scream as the bike hurtles down the slope.

This is the moment I wait for each day.

The moment of free fall.

The moment of rapidly changing perceptions.

Everything becomes nothing.

All becomes none.

This is the moment of knowing that a sacrifice to one may be a simple matter of choice to another.

And so, I choose. I choose to be with Aarash now, flying down this bike path that cuts through the heart of Burlington, the sun and the wind kissing our faces.

Look at Aarash, free to be himself, with no pressing need to lose himself first only to spend a lifetime retracing his path to his lost self.

Everything is already *just right*, right here, right now. Why do we need to ruin it and then spend this one life trying to make it *just right* all over again?

7

____

"I don't want to be a person. I want to be a cat," Aarash says at breakfast and proceeds to lick the scrambled eggs off his plate.

It is already tomorrow here in Belvenia Road. It always astounds me how the days fly by and crawl at the same time. My little one is not so little anymore. He is beginning to have aspirations now.

"What do you like about being a cat?" I ask.

"Hmm … I just like being a cat."

"I wonder if cats like going to the beach. What do you think?"

"You were walking with a cat the other day at the beach," he reminds me.

"Which cat? Which other day?"

"One day, a very long time ago, Mumma, Aarash, and Cindy went to the beach." Aarash turns storyteller now. So here comes a dramatic pause.

"And then what happened?"

"All three of us played in the water together. And we had a lot of fun. The end."

"That sounds swell," I say. "Would you like Cindy to come to the beach with us one day? Maybe we could ask her."

"Of course!" Aarash hops off his chair and proceeds to grab his slippers.

"Now?"

"Yes, let's go, Mumma!" He pulls his slippers on, places my pair by the door, and waits for me.

"Okay." I try to sound more enthused than alarmed by this sudden urge for socialization that my nearly-three-year-old is exhibiting.

"And maybe, she can tell me how to become a cat," Aarash muses.

HIDE-AND-SEEK

HIDE-AND-SEEK

Every child's favourite game. One mother's worst nightmare.

In a seemingly endless game of hide-and-seek, a mother looks for her child in all his favourite hiding spots. But he has hidden himself so well she's unable to find him.

Then she comes up with the perfect bait to coax him out. His favourite toys!

Will they entice him to reveal himself? Or has she been playing the wrong game all along?

Hide-and-Seek secured an Honourable Mention in the Spring/Summer 2021 issue of Allegory Magazine, Volume 39/66.

1

$\mathcal{Y}$ou've become terrific at playing hide-and-seek.

There was a time, not too long ago, when you were only too eager to give yourself away. A not-so-muffled giggle. A deliberately conspicuous thump. A noisy swish of fabric.

And when all else failed, I only had to ask, "Where are you?", and the shape of you would burst into view. Like a dolphin leaping, breaking the surface of the ocean, you'd plunge into the void of your absence, shouting, "Here!", and career into my arms.

"Where are you?" I holler now. My voice is hoarse from all the times I've called out to you since morning.

You remain quiet and hidden, as if you have finally understood the rules of the game and discovered a compulsive urge to abide by them.

2

———

Six months before you were born, I started to read aloud to you every day, determined to pass on my love of words to you. *Possum Magic* and a slew of other books by Mem Fox. *Room On The Broom* by Julia Donaldson.

When you were ten months old, you decided that books were for ripping pages from. That was when I learnt about board books and the importance of storing newspapers and pamphlets instead of tossing them into the bin unread.

When you were two years old, you paused me in the middle of a reading of a *Thomas the Tank Engine* story and asked, "How can we go inside this book?"

I stared at you for a few moments, awed by the simple sincerity on your face. And while you waited patiently for a reply, I swallowed all the words that threatened to tumble out of my mouth, for none was worthy of constituting a response to your innocence.

"How can we go inside this book?" you asked again, misconstruing my silence for inattention. "We need to find a way," you insisted, devouring the images of the shiny red and bright blue and gleaming green trains puffing busily around the island of Sodor.

"Well," I said, "take a good look at the pictures. Then close your eyes and you'll see all the trains in your mind."

Lame, I know. It didn't fool you either.

I look for you now in your reading nook under the bottom shelf of your closet.

A blue plush mat covers most of the floor and a small beige pillow with the image of an orange fox on its cover rests on it. A teddy rests against the pillow and a reading lamp looms over it.

All your picture books lie scattered in this space, some open to well-thumbed pages. I resist the urge to snap them shut and stack them in a neat pile. What if you've indeed found a way to slip inside any of them and are still working your way out?

3
_____

When you were not really two anymore but also not yet three, and I resolutely refrained from referring to you as an almost-three-year-old for I didn't want time to hurtle any faster than it already was, you asked me what monsters and ghosts were.

Had we just read *The Monster Under The Shed*, a Thomas the Tank Engine tale? Or was it Brigitte Weninger's *Davy, Help! It's a Ghost!*

I recall neither which book it was nor my answer, which surely must have been inept, for it didn't take you long to figure out that whatever or whoever they were, real or imagined, monsters and ghosts were something to be terrified of.

I look for you under my bed, a place you believed would never be invaded by anything petrifying. Dust bunnies and cobwebs shiver like drifting mist under my laborious breath.

Even through their haze, I can see your little yellow excavator is gone. A-ha! So you did sneak in here, after all.

I hurry downstairs and rummage in your toybox. A sleek, red convertible catches my eye. I grab it and run back up and slip it like an offering under my bed.

4

---

hen you were three, you asked me about God. Actually, no. You asked me why the church bells rang. Despite my convent school education, I didn't know much about churches, and I told you so. "Why?" you asked.

Later that evening, after you had fallen fast asleep, I opened the boxes in the basement until I found the one I was looking for. The next morning, you noticed the tiny altar I had set up in a corner of the kitchen.

The Gods of my childhood are exotic. One has the face and tail of a monkey. Another has the head of an elephant.

One has indigo skin and a peacock feather in his crown. "Blue person," you observed.

Another wears a cobra as a necklace.

Nestled in the congregation of idols and framed images on the altar was a standing crucifix, an acquisition from my convent school days.

I told you the names of all those Gods and whatever little of their stories I knew. And I also told you those were merely stories. People like to make up stories about everything and everyone unfamiliar to them.

God is as real as *Thomas the Tank Engine* could ever be, I explained, pleased with my deployment of simile.

"Like monsters and ghosts," you chimed in.

5

When you were four, you asked me about death. Yet again, I talked to you about the myriad stories people make up about death and all that comes beyond it.

But this time, with much more conviction than I had been able to muster in our discussions about monsters and ghosts and Gods, I said to you, "No one really knows what happens when we die. Anyone who tells you otherwise is lying."

"But we can imagine?" you suggested and asked at the same time.

"Sure. Maybe we become stars?"

"Maybe we become trees?"

"Maybe our bodies become part of the earth and help other things grow." And I wondered if the residual ashes of cremated bodies could help sustain new life too.

After a few days of silence on the topic, you declared, "I know what happens after we die, Mumma."

You were trying to put on your shoes by yourself and I was

sitting on the floor beside you, hands clasped together, trying hard to resist the uncontrollable urge to help you.

"What happens?" I asked, doubling my efforts at maintaining a façade of patience and calm.

"We come back again," you said.

"That could very well be," I said, determined to accept your hypothesis but also not completely eliminate its inherent uncertainty.

"That is how it is, Mumma," you insisted. "I know. We come back as another person. We always come back."

And I had to concede you may have somehow coaxed a secret from the very belly of this Universe.

6

———————

The creek where it happened is the last place I search, convinced you wouldn't come back to the very spot where we had inadvertently begun our unending game of hide-and-seek, your turn to hide and mine to seek, and you had simply vanished. I didn't expect to find you here but now that you are nowhere in sight, I am sorely disappointed.

Gloomy clouds have gathered on the horizon and they now soar towards me. The distant rumble of thunder rolls across the sky like a landslide.

Everyone thinks lightning doesn't strike the same place twice, but it does. It did the last time we were here, in this very place where I now lie spread-eagled like an X marking the spot where the only treasure I ever had was last seen alive and has since vanished.

A part of me wishes to hang around and see if lightning will strike here a third time now, so I will never need to think or do anything ever again because I am so tired, I am so, so tired, but another part of me insists I must run back home before the storm arrives because I still haven't found you and our game is not over yet.

7

Are ghosts for real?
Does God exist?
What happens to us when we die?
Funny how I am the one with all the questions and you are the one with all the answers now.

8

Sleep eludes me all night. In the brief flashes of illumination that lightning brings, I keep my eyes peeled for you. But no shadows move, no unexplained silhouettes appear.

When the storm passes at the break of dawn, I will myself off the bed and peek under.

Et voila! The red convertible has disappeared!

Hope propels me down the stairs and I throw open your toybox, wondering if I should place your next offering somewhere more visible to me, so I can watch you come in to fetch it.

But there they are. Atop the little jumble of vehicles you gleaned endless delight from, lie your yellow excavator and red convertible. Did you put them back last night? Or have they been lying here since the last time you and I cleaned up and put away your toys before bedtime?

I fall down, my legs having abruptly forgotten their function to hold me up. My heart aches so much I think it will explode and I want it to. I want it to stop beating, stop trying so hard to keep me alive.

I turn to one side and curl into a foetal position, the way you were cocooned in my womb all those months when I came up with false pretexts to schedule ultrasound appointments just so I could see you even when you were hidden inside of me.

At first, you were a mere flash of blinking light, which the technician declared was your beating heart. Months later, your spine unfurled like a railway track.

At every visit, your heartbeat was like the gallop of a racehorse, as if somehow even back then, even before you were born, you knew you'd zip through this lifetime at the speed of lightning.

Sleep finally arrives as an accomplice to exhaustion.

As I give in, yearning to be completely deprived of all thought and sensation, something presses into the small of my back and reminds me of the way your knees would push into me in the middle of the night as you'd try to curl yourself into a ball and snuggle up to me at the same time.

Something else rakes my hair gently like an extraordinarily wide-toothed comb, and I do what I've always done whenever your fingers have sought out a comforter.

I lift my head and without turning back, I untie my ponytail and bunch it back into a bun I pile atop my head. The familiar tug resumes as something prods and holds on to my bun and after a few moments, whatever it is, finally rests, unstirring, in peace, warm and gentle, beside me.

9

———

"**A**re you OK?" This was the one question you never liked me asking you.

The last time you told me off for hurling this question your way was when we had gone to pay our neighbour, two doors down, a brief visit, and her dog, Daisy, burst across their threshold and barrelled into your chest as if she were meeting a long lost lover.

You stood patiently as Daisy sniffed and licked and nudged you, perhaps wishing her paws would somehow morph into arms she could wrap around you. You were only a child's head taller than she was.

Our neighbour pulled Daisy back and I bent to ask you, "Are you OK?" You deigned to answer that question with only a slight nod.

When we returned home, you admonished me, "If I don't say anything, it means I am OK."

10

I won't ask if it is you.

I won't ask if you are OK.

To give in to the urge to verify is to admit doubt. To believe without demanding any more evidence is to have faith.

If I don't seek you anymore, perhaps you will no longer feel the need to hide.

THE GIFT OF TIME

THE GIFT OF TIME

Time! Ah, that slippery measure of our lives! Which parent would turn down a generous offer of a little more time in their day?

Not Myra. Single mom. Immigrant. Hobbyist painter.

Myra unexpectedly finds the gift of time in an ordinary-looking mirror that cost her ten bucks. She steps into it for a much needed mid-day snooze when her little boy, Arjun, is away at school. She steps out to find that no time has lapsed in the real world in the meantime.

That additional time to rest and recover makes her a much better parent, she finds. And she is grateful for it.

Until Arjun stumbles into the mirror one day, leaving Myra with no choice but to figure out with great urgency what price the mirror will extract from her for its gift of time.

Because sometimes, in life and in magic, there is no such thing as a free gift.

~

1

———

The mirror had cost only ten dollars. Ten bucks for a full-length mirror. That itself should have been a dead giveaway. The first indicator that it was something someone wanted to be rid of.

Myra had inspected it thoroughly at the store. Its back was made of thin cardboard. The front had been wrapped in a milky plastic sheet, which had blurred her reflection.

It had a narrow white frame, certainly not made of wood. What it was made of, she couldn't tell. Something lightweight. She had been able to tuck it under one arm and walk out of the store to her car, guiding the shopping cart in front with her other hand while Arjun, her four-year-old, had pushed it.

All the other mirrors in the aisle had cost at least ten times as much. She hadn't given them a second glance. This one had been a fortuitous steal. She'd have been a fool to not buy it. Besides, she could always return it if it turned out to be one of those fun house mirrors that twisted you into ghoulish shapes.

Putting up the mirror on the wall beside the window in

their sole bedroom had proven to be yet another unexpectedly easy task. Two holes drilled into the wall. Two nails hammered into them. And up the mirror had gone.

There. Now she wouldn't have to prop her little boy up on the edge of the washbasin every time he wished to see himself from head to toe.

But the funny thing was that Arjun had not cared much for the mirror in their bedroom after it had gone up. That should have been the second sign that something was amiss.

Arjun had been genuinely excited at the store. He was the one who had pointed out the mirror to Myra in the first place, reminding her of a long-ago promise she had made to furnish the bedroom with a mirror.

Something that would ensure he never forgot how beautiful he was. Something that would remind her too, over and over again, how beautiful she was.

But once the plastic had been peeled away and the mirror had been nailed to the wall, Arjun behaved as if the damned thing didn't exist. Not a peek into it. Not even a sideways glance.

Even though the mirror reflected his beautiful self in the truest way possible. No distortions in shape or shade. Which had been a pleasant surprise, considering how cheap it had been.

But it wasn't until two days later that Myra caught a glimpse of what the mirror could actually do.

2

———

t was Thursday night, and she was exhausted. Arjun had slept poorly this past week, waking Myra several times during the night. For water. He was thirsty. Or to push away the blanket. It was too hot. Or to ask for a blanket again. It was too cold.

After each interruption to the night, the child promptly drifted back into deep sleep, but Myra remained awake. Her body was overwhelmingly tired but her mind, once aroused, couldn't settle itself back into slumber.

When she closed her eyes, the sounds of the night amplified around her. The incessant ticking of the two-dollar clock from IKEA. The whisper of Arjun's breathing.

That was when she first heard it.

A soft fluttery sound. A gentle *rat-a-tat-tat-tat*. Interspersed with purrs. It seemed to come from the blinds on the window.

Myra lay in the dark, listening to it, wondering if it would let up.

It didn't.

A brief pause, here and there.

And then it resumed.

She reached for the bedside lamp and switched it on. The sound ceased.

She switched the lamp off and sank back into the mattress. Within a moment, the sound resumed.

Rat-a-tat-tat-tat. Rat-a-tat-tat-tat. A gentle clicking. Then *purrrr, purrrr.*

She switched the lamp on again and, like before, the sound ceased instantly in response. Night insects, perhaps. A moth on the window. Spiders mating.

She glanced at the clock on the wall. Two o'clock. Shen turned the lamp off and slumped back into bed, dreading the imminent arrival of a new day.

Arjun would be awake by five in the morning. Five-thirty at most. And Myra would have to drag herself through yet another day, nursing a nasty headache from lack of sleep, high on caffeine, and prone to irritation. The mere thought made her want to cry.

Tears filled her eyes like shiny things in the dark, obfuscating her view of the night beyond. She rubbed them away with the heels of her palms. Which is why she didn't see the strange light creep in and light up the room in a dim glow. When she opened her eyes, the room shimmered with muted light.

Myra had seen that light before. Every morning at six-thirty when the neighbour pulled their car out of their driveway. Light from the vehicle's headlamps spilled into the bedroom through the nearly closed slats and around the edges of the window blinds, swept through every inch of darkness, and probed every corner to tease out everything that wanted to remain hidden in the shadows.

Another sleepless soul, Myra thought sadly. It was only a momentary glow though. One that moved through the expanse of the room for a couple of moments, casting a slatted dance of light and shadow, and left just as quickly as it had come.

But this glow did not move. It stayed, as if it had come from within the room. It flickered on occasion, like a candle flame wobbling on its wick.

Myra looked towards the window, and realized the light was not coming through it. It was coming from the mirror beside the window.

It took her a few more moments to comprehend the thought that had just formed in her mind.

The light came from the mirror. Not the window.

From the other side of the mirror. Not from the other side of the window.

Both were surfaces of glass. One was transparent. The other was reflective.

One could let light through. The other couldn't. At least, it shouldn't.

Later, Myra would wonder why she hadn't felt afraid for herself, or for Arjun, at the first sight of light pouring inexplicably out of a mirror.

Later, she would tell herself that she had always known there was something unusual about the mirror, something a little off, for who in their right mind would sell a full-length mirror, with an almost-rare capacity for perfect reflection, for only ten dollars?

Or maybe, she'd rationalize later, she had read so many

picture books to Arjun in his four years of life on earth that very few things took her by surprise anymore. She had seen it all.

Flying cars. Talking owls. Holes dug through the centre of the earth and beyond. Dogs blasted off into space. Dinosaurs ferrying children to school. Donkeys wearing underpants on their heads.

After all that, a glowing mirror could hardly rattle her.

That night, she was merely inquisitive. Curious, she rolled out of bed, walked up to the mirror, and peered into it from the side. Only her craning face peered back at her. Bright and clear.

It took her a few moments to comprehend she was seeing something she shouldn't have been able to.

The room was dark, save for that dim glow. To any outside observer, she'd be nothing more than a silhouette. A deeper darkness carved out of night-space. Only the whites of her eyes should have been visible. This is what her mirror should have shown her too.

Instead, her mirror-self glowed. Her mirror-room shone a little, as if lit up from within, sharing some of its own light, no matter how feeble, with the rest of the world. A gleam in the dark. A glow-worm.

Cool, Myra thought. It didn't occur to her then that this was unusual behaviour for a mirror in real life.

She straightened up and positioned herself directly in front of the mirror. So did her reflection. Without warning, tiny points of light sparkled and pricked and shimmered in the mirror all around her reflection.

She reached out a hand and pressed it on the mirror, half-hoping it would give way and she'd go tumbling into a Narnia that had somehow opened its doors only for her.

Nothing happened.

The glass was as solid and unyielding as the wall beside it.

Disappointed, she peeled herself away from the mirror and tucked herself into bed once again. She turned to her side and gently ran her fingers through her child's hair. He liked to wear it long.

Tears rolled down her cheeks. More than four years had passed since Arjun's birth, yet Myra found herself breaking into unexpected tears more often than not.

Her baby was growing up too fast. Myra wanted to stop time in any which way possible, bring it to a screeching halt, the rest of the world be damned, for all she wanted was to trap herself and her child in this moment of innocence, in this moment of early childhood where magic and wonder prevailed. But time was running past relentlessly, as if it were desperate to get away from the here and now, as if it were in a real hurry to go someplace else, become something else.

Also, she needed to sleep. The tears spilled readily when she had been neglecting her own self for too long. She hadn't slept well in days. She had been subsisting on leftovers and snacks, even though she heaped Arjun's plate and lunchbox with fresh fruits and rainbow-coloured meals.

The unremarkable ordinariness of the mirror was the last straw. She should have known better than to seek magic in a cheap mirror.

Even the whole wide world, with its collective wisdom on living and parenting, often seemed so devoid of beauty and magic. How could a mere piece of glass be any different?

3
____

For two nights, Myra made a conscious effort to
be in bed by half-past eight, so she could sleep
when Arjun slept and wake up alongside him at five the next
morning.

This meant she couldn't catch the latest episode of
Murdoch Mysteries right when it aired on CBC TV. Eight
o'clock on Monday nights. That would have to wait until
Saturday afternoon to coincide with Arjun's designated
weekly TV time.

Netflix binges had long become an alien concept to her.
When she spent four or five hours at night enjoying episode
after episode of *Bridgerton* and then made do with barely two
or three hours of sleep, she typically spent the next day being
an irate mother, snapping at her four-year-old when he
insisted on wearing his socks all by himself, even if it meant
he'd be late for school.

She didn't want to be an angry mother like the one she'd
had. She wanted to be a good mother, an epitome of calm, a

personification of gentle grace, a parent who role-modelled emotional maturity, and not emotional distress, to her child.

And for the most part, she managed to pull it off. So long as she slept well, ate well, made small but steady progress on the collection of paintings she had begun working on two months ago, she felt fulfilled.

From that well of contentment sprung unconditional love for her and for Arjun, a child who was a natural delight. She wanted to be a safe place for him to express himself, his entire range of emotions and thoughts.

When she was present and attentive to his needs and her own, she was a great mother, a parent who adored her child, who found everything about this little human utterly fascinating.

The only trouble was it was all boring as hell. The entire ordinary, predictable routine.

Waking up with Arjun. Enjoying a fun morning routine of breakfast and packing lunch and getting ready for school. Dropping him off.

Coming back home, now serene and peaceful, the entire space stirring her creativity. Losing herself for a few hours in her artwork. The act of creation filling her up in a way even motherhood could not.

Taking some time in the afternoon to enjoy a cup of tea. Preparing dinner.

Picking up Arjun. Enjoying the drive back home, enchanted with all his tales of a busy day at school.

Relishing dinnertime with him. Cleaning up. Bathing her child. Reading to him. Realizing he has fallen asleep mid-reading, head on her chest.

Peeling herself away from under him. Shifting him to a more comfortable position. Pulling the blanket up to his chin.

Gazing at his innocent face, watching the subtle rise and fall of his blanket in rhythm with the movement of his chest under it. Whispering to her sleeping child how grateful she was to have him in her life. Acknowledging what a privilege it was.

Realizing how perfect her life had become, how easy it had been to make her life perfect.

Conceding that when she was happy, Arjun was happy too, safe in the knowledge that his home, his haven was not under any threat of mutating out of its current comfortable form anytime soon.

Castigating herself, out of habit, for not being able to hold on to this perfection, for always letting it slip away just as easily as it made its way back into her life.

Stepping into the shower or running a warm bath for herself. Meditating for twenty minutes right after. Tucking herself into bed right next to Arjun. Falling asleep in time to ensure a good eight hours or more of uninterrupted rest.

Waking up just a few minutes before her little one did. Beginning the day by gifting herself the space and time to prepare. Prepare to surrender, prepare to bend like water and flow, no matter what the day presented to them.

4

———————

Typically, she was able to keep up this routine for three days, or four at most. Then something would pat her on the back and tell her, "Good job! You've earned your rest now. You deserve a break."

And then she'd be right back on Netflix, prowling through the endless web of trailers in the hour right before she'd have to go and pick Arjun up from school, forsaking her cup of afternoon tea and deciding between leftovers and takeout for dinner, salivating at the sight of all those other worlds, beckoning to her, their doorways opening wide, luring her inside, so she could lose herself and escape from the reality that her life had become, a reality that felt like it would never change.

The reality of routine, of prediction, of monotony. Of utter, unimaginable sameness.

The sky steeped in the same, unchanging blue. Leaf-buds swelling obscenely like hard nipples on springtime branches. Tulips and daffodils blooming on the lawns of neighbours who had too much time on their hands and too little imagination in their heads.

It was all maddeningly mediocre. Like a magic trick she had seen so often it had lost all its charm even though she still hadn't figured out how it all worked. Surely, she deserved a break.

And that would be the night everything would come crashing down again.

A late-night Netflix binge. Falling asleep at three. Waking up at five. Spending the day like a bear with a sore head. Brushing away her four-year-old every time he asked her to play with him. Pain exploding through her head.

Arjun putting up a brave front at first. Arjun eventually beginning to whine, surely sensing something amiss in her, in their home, something that had been so perfect only last evening, something that had disappeared overnight, and who knew if it will ever come back again.

Guilt coursing through her veins, terror of all the anxiety she was filling him up with, shame for all the parenting failures she was committing now, mistakes that would surely come back to haunt her in the years to come.

Wondering how it had all come to this. Cursing herself for not being able to do the simple things. Eating. Conversing. Chilling out.

Switching on *Paw Patrol* on the TV to keep her little one occupied, to keep him away from her. Promising herself she'd resume her routine of going to bed no later than half-past eight tonight.

Feeling infuriated that she couldn't even allow herself a sliver of entertainment.

Feeling mad at her child for turning her world upside down.

Feeling incensed by the knowledge that Nick, her ex-husband, now blessedly child-free, was soaking up the sunshine in Hawaii with his latest girlfriend.

Feeling irate at her parents whom she had left behind in another continent for the sake of a man who had left *her* behind in turn, unwilling to be saddled with a child, whose grandparents were loathe to travel halfway across the world to help care for their only grandchild.

Feeling terrified that after all her attempts to ensure otherwise, she was indeed turning into her own mother.

Feeling abandoned by society and the government and the institution of marriage, all abstract concepts that made promises they never kept.

Wishing this day would end right now.

Wishing she could simply crawl back under the covers and sleep. Sleep, sleep, and sleep until eternity.

5

____

An offering.

The idea came to Myra a few days later when Arjun said he'd like to visit a temple to see what God was all about (an idea planted into his head by his faraway grandparents), and she had insisted on first purchasing fresh flowers and fruits to offer to the deities. A customary practice she did not believe in but had felt obliged to pass on knowledge of to her son, for him to decide whether or not it was worth following.

The offering had to be of value, she decided, not necessarily financial but something that bore some significance to her. A price that was immeasurable.

She chose one of her early paintings. A watercolour she had conjured to life for pleasure, for fun, before years of education and expert advice had sullied her creativity and rendered her art predictable, jaded.

Now she was unlearning what she had learnt. Trying to regain the spontaneity she had lost, keenly aware of the irony inherent in such an endeavour.

She hadn't even framed her work, refusing to confine it any more than the paper itself did, the archival paper on which she had painted a brook, tumbling blithely towards an unseen destination, meandering through a green meadow in the shade of summertime trees, birds and butterflies darting about, drawing streaks of colours in the air around them, white clouds adrift, breaking up the sameness of the blue sky, and the sun generously warm but not too hot on this beautiful day.

Blue skies and white clouds. For as long as she could remember, they had been undeniable images of happiness. The sight of fluffy white clouds drifting in a blue sky filled her heart with an inexplicable lightness, as if she too could fly, for somehow the sight of them had helped her shed the onus she had been carrying, the burden of living.

Or maybe that had been the picture of happiness planted in her head by Enid Blyton. The summertime escapades of the *Famous Five* had become Myra's own in her childhood.

She used to imagine herself as George, fierce and courageous, diving headlong into the most dangerous of adventures, refusing to be limited by gender stereotyping.

But look at Myra now! Keeping house like Anne. Sweet, domestic Anne.

That realization had stolen her love for blue skies and white clouds. The sight of them no longer bewitched her.

Clutching her painting in her hands, she stood in front of the mirror. It was early afternoon. Half-past one. Sunlight streamed into the bedroom through the south-facing window adjacent to the mirror. A light lunch and two espressos had done little to keep exhaustion at bay. Drowsiness clung to her as if it had nowhere else to go.

But she couldn't afford the luxury of sleep now. In less than two hours, she'd need to pick Arjun up from school. Several mothers on the internet swore by power naps. But Myra worried that if she were to close her eyes now, she'd be dead to the world for days.

Her mirror-self smiled and held out her hand. Myra presented her painting to the mirror, brushing it lightly against the surface of the glass. At the lightest touch, her painting was whisked into the mirror and out of sight.

In an explosion of soundless light, the mirror opened itself to her, its glow billowing out and engulfing her until she stepped forward and entered the world behind the mirror, without quite seeing where it began and where her own room ended.

Sprawling meadows unfurled at her feet and met a lazy blue sky at the horizon. A brook burbled beside where she stood. A cardinal sang from somewhere above her, coaxing new leaves to spring forth. The fragrance of unnamed wildflowers tickled her nose, lingering briefly before disappearing into the aether once more.

Soft grass kissed her bare feet as she took one step, then another, breathing in the dewy scent of the clean air around her.

She came upon a picnic mat, held in place by stones on three corners while the fourth corner flapped occasionally in the cool breeze. She sank into the centre of the mat and lay down on her back. The sun was a little behind her, out of sight, but her limbs relaxed in his generous warmth.

She closed her eyes and succumbed to sleep.

6

Myra awoke slowly. She stirred to the scents and sounds around her, reluctant to open her eyes. The cardinal whistled sweetly. A warm breeze soothed her body. The stream gurgled like a baby.

It reminded her of Arjun, when he was a baby, so content to remain in her arms, yet to rise to the bait of the world outside.

Mumma! A distant shout jarred her out of her reverie.

Arjun! She opened her eyes and sat up so quickly she almost pulled a muscle in her back. Her child was nowhere to be seen.

Was he still at school? She had no idea how long she had been asleep for. A heavy sense of dread squeezed her heart and made her gasp. She looked around. The sun still shone behind her, almost exactly where it had been when she had fallen asleep. Perhaps she had had only a power nap after all?

Then the next thought nagged her. How was she to get back to her world? She looked up the way she had come, and sure enough, the air in the distance shimmered like a mirage. A sheer curtain fluttering in the wind. A veil between worlds.

She jumped up and hurtled towards it, heart in mouth, afraid it would disappear before she could reach it.

But it didn't. It opened up as she approached it. A great chasm. A vast nothingness.

She leapt into it and tumbled onto the floor in their bedroom. Her back twinged once more. Argh! She was getting too old for these antics.

She first sought the clock on the wall. Half-past one. Half-past one? She shook her head, frantic. Had the clock stopped working? But no, the second hand was still spinning and ticking.

The room swam around her. She put a hand to her head as if she needed to hold it in place, lest it should fall down and roll away from her body, so utterly discombobulated was she.

The second hand swept past the number twelve. The minute hand lurched forward. A strangled cry of relief, of hope, escaped Myra's lips.

She looked into the mirror, and there was her mirror-self, smiling at her, a calm witness to Myra's confusion, a source of assurance that whatever had transpired this afternoon, no harm had been done.

With a renewed burst of energy in her limbs, Myra changed into a pair of jeans and a button-down shirt, grabbed her phone and purse and keys, and dashed out the door like a woman possessed.

The springtime sun in her world was still high up in the sky, she noticed without quite registering the fact. It was only when she pulled into the parking lot of Arjun's school that she paused to think for a moment.

Several cars were parked in the sprawling lot. Teachers' cars. On the basketball court beyond the school building, a group of older children played under the supervision of a grown-up. A coach, from the looks of it.

A few more groups of children were playing in different parts of the grassy grounds that unfurled behind the main school building. She squinted her eyes to see if Arjun was among them, but the children were too far away for her to identify him or his classmates.

She scrutinized the school building. Windows had been thrown open in some of the classes. An invitation to the warm breeze.

Myra rolled down the car window, and the unmistakable buzz of a busy day at school thrummed the air around her. Indecipherable shouts. An occasional whistle, like that of a referee's. The general hum of activity and sound that busy children seemed to emanate all the time, no matter what they were up to, except perhaps when they fell asleep.

She picked up her phone, her hands shaking with relief and confusion. It was nearly two in the afternoon. Arjun's school wouldn't draw to a close for at least another hour and a half. Surely, he must be inside too. But she had to make sure.

When one of the admin assistants at the school answered her call, Myra said, "Hi, this is Ms. Raman. My child, Arjun, is in JK."

"Of course, Ms. Raman, what can I do for you?" The lady pronounced it as 'ramen'.

Myra hadn't known what she'd say but the pretext now came to her glibly, as if it had been sitting on the tip of her tongue all along, merely waiting for her permission to roll off.

"Arjun was a little upset this morning at drop-off," she

explained. "He hasn't been sleeping well these past few nights. I had promised to swing by at around two to see if he was doing OK or if he'd like to come back home early today."

"Sure, I'll take a look for you."

Myra didn't have to wait long.

"Nothing to worry about, Ms. Raman. He's playing with his friends now. It's free play time for them and their class teacher has taken them outdoors. She says he's had a great day so far. Would you still like to pick him up now?"

Relief flooded Myra's body. "That's OK. I'll come back at the usual pick-up time. Thank you for checking."

She had more than an hour to spare. She drove to the nearest Starbucks, grabbed a tall hazelnut latte, and made her way down to the beach, a fifteen-minute drive away from Arjun's school.

And there she sat on the sand, soft and grainy now, not hard and clumpy like it had been a fortnight ago when the city had still been in the grip of one of the coldest winters on record. The great lake was placid. Small waves of water gently brushed against the shore and retreated without fuss.

And there she sat and thought and thought about the mirror, that cheap ten-dollar purchase, that had somehow led her into a different world where time stood still.

7
———

Growing up, Myra had been sensible and lucky enough to steer clear of the trap of addiction.

But now, as a single parent, she had been so deprived of sleep for so long she thought she'd give anything, anything barring her life and that of her only child, to get some sleep.

Deep, uninterrupted sleep. More precisely, some *time* to sleep well.

When Arjun was away at school, there were so many things she had to attend to that sleep was a luxury she could ill afford in his absence.

But now the mirror had solved this conundrum for her. Since that fateful afternoon, she had taken to stepping daily into the mirror-world, still a panorama of meadows and brook and blue sky and white clouds, and had fallen into deep sleep easily, assuredly.

Each time, she had woken up gently, slowly, and had walked through that crevice in space back into their bedroom to find that time in the real world had held its breath, waiting patiently for her to return, before it could resume its forward march once again.

It was such a perfect arrangement that she tried as hard as she could to keep the doubts at bay. They'd come eventually, she knew that for a fact. But for now, she tried to take things slowly, keep them simple.

She set a few ground rules for herself.

First, she would use the mirror only when she was alone at home.

Typically, in the afternoon hours that stretched languidly between lunch hour and pick-up time. That was when she felt most drowsy. Slumber then became an extravagant treat, rendered all the more enjoyable and rejuvenating when it followed an entire morning dedicated to her art.

Second, she would not make Arjun privy to the mirror's magic.

She still didn't know enough about the mirror and its workings to introduce an impressionable child to its enigma. Perhaps, some day when he was old enough, some day when he had children of his own and yearned for restful sleep, she would pass on the mirror to him like a family heirloom. For now, it was best he remained in the dark. He showed the mirror so little interest anyway she had no intentions of drawing his attention back to it.

Third, she would not enter the mirror at night.

For one thing, that would be in violation of her first rule. She was never alone at home at night-time. Arjun was in bed every night, and even if slipping into the mirror meant she'd be back before another moment had passed in the real world, it was a risk not worth taking. The possibility, no matter how slight, that Arjun might wake up in the dark of the night, find himself alone, and call out to his mother only to realize she had gone missing, was so terrifying that she had no intentions of ever tempting fate in this matter.

For another, she knew from a lifetime of living that the world at night was vastly different than at daytime. The creatures that came out at night never revealed themselves in the light of the day. Nature must have had her reasons for keeping apart the lives of diurnal and nocturnal creatures. Unless Myra could determine if the mirror-world too separated night and day, she was content with all that it offered her. Eternal sunshine to sleep in as the rest of the world came to a halt.

The most gratifying outcome of this development was that she had become the perfect mom. Well-rested, she was calm and collected every moment of the day she spent with Arjun.

He was already such a sweet child. On those rare occasions when impulse took over and he kicked his shoes away, frustrated at not being able to tie his own laces, or threw his coat down, unable to put it up on a hanger, or sat on the floor and cried for half an hour, bogged down by a long day of mental stimulation and physical exertion at school, Myra became the kind of parent every child needed.

Graceful under pressure. Calm in the face of her child's storm. Role-modelling empathy and equanimity in the most difficult of situations.

Not even feeling the urge to shush her child or rush him through his feelings or wishing he'd stop crying. No. None of those primal urges that drive parents crazy because what they want is the impossible—for their child to never have to encounter pain.

Instead, she became the parent she had always wanted to

be, and better still, she found that now she could be this parent all the time. This Zen parent, who'd never again turn into an angry, yelling mumzilla, the default state of most sleep-deprived caregivers, the state that she too lapsed into occasionally back in the day, before the mirror had graced her bedroom wall.

Even now, the memory of her lapses of composure wrecked her with guilt. After every outburst, when sanity was eventually restored, she worried that these lapses alone would cost her child much, much more than he'd gain in emotional health by her peaceful parenting practice at all other times.

She shook her head to brush that thought away. Why dwell on a past that would never repeat itself? She had found a cure to sleep deprivation.

And even the phantom baby cries she had been hearing since the day Arjun was born, like a horrible case of tinnitus, had disappeared. Whoever knew that just the right amount of sleep and rest could make a world of difference in their lives?

The fourth ground rule she set was this: she must attempt to determine the price she has to pay for this magic.

It was not a rule per se, but Myra had never been one to sponge off others, let alone a magic mirror. So far, the mirror had only been giving her the gift of time to do with as she pleased. She always chose to sleep. She had given the mirror only her cherished painting, which had come to life in this hidden world. The gift she had given had been imbued with magic and gifted back to her again.

The more she thought about it, the more uncomfortable she grew, although not enough to quit stepping into the mirror for her early afternoon naps. Like a smoker who derived guilty pleasure from each drag, each puff, worrying on one hand when the death knell would sound but opting for instant gratification in lieu of longevity and good health, which even abstinence could never truly guarantee.

Myra too had grown accustomed and addicted to those bonus hours of sleep. She could no longer imagine getting through a day without them.

This was especially true on weekends and on school holidays when Arjun was at home all day. Unless he was away at camp or at a friend's place, Myra was compelled to wait for the next opportunity to slip into the mirror without being missed or noticed.

But knowing there was an end to this wait, seeing the flicker of light at the end of the tunnel was all the impetus she needed to keep going.

But she needed to know what she'd be asked to forfeit when the time came. The more she enjoyed this precious gift of time, the more she worried she might be asked to pay an inconceivable price for it.

8

———————

*A*rjun wanted to become Aria when he was six.

It all began when his cousins crossed the pond to visit them that summer. His maternal uncle, aunt, and cousins —seven-year-old Priya and eleven-year-old Sunny—had come and stayed with them for a fortnight.

What a ball they'd all had! Mornings at the beach. Afternoons in the backyard. Evenings at playgrounds in the neighbourhood. Nights spent falling asleep gazing at stars in the backyard, although every morning they somehow woke up in the comfortable bed in the bedroom Arjun still shared with his mother, co-sleeping the only form of sleeping he had ever known since he was born.

But what struck him most about their visit was Priya's wonderful, colourful attire. Frocks and skirts, frilly tops and sporty tights, hairbands and ribbons. She was a rainbow, so many and varied and vivid were the colours she wore.

For some reason, Arjun had had the sense to wait until his cousins had gone back across the pond to approach his mother with the desire that had been burning in his little six-year-old heart. "Can I wear a skirt, please?"

Myra, that perfect mother, that all-accepting parent whose only mission in life was to ensure she stayed out of her son's way, hugged him in response and said, "Why, of course, sweetie!"

The first frock she bought for him was a pink-and-orange affair, one small step towards change. Arjun loved it.

He first wore it on a day in late-August summer, when the sun was still high in the sky and the bedroom, with its south-facing windows, was flooded with bright light. He wore it and twirled in front of the mirror, delighted with the swish and the swirl of the fabric, the way the colours danced in his reflection.

And his mirror-self smiled at him. He paused mid-twirl, but his mirror-self continued to whirl.

Eyes wide with curiosity, he stepped closer to the mirror. His mirror-self paused in his dance, then moved closer to him too.

Arjun pressed a hand on the mirror. His mirror-self did too.

The glass shivered and shimmered, like ripples on the face of a lake.

Arjun's hand passed through the glass, now a soft, grey nothingness. Another hand clasped his. Certainly, his mirror-self's.

Without a moment's hesitation, he slipped through.

9

Myra was waiting for the coffee machine to fill her cup when, for the briefest of moments, the world around her came crashing to a standstill.

Only for a moment. Not even.

An insignificant pause in the earth's revolution around the sun. As if the unstoppable planet had encountered a little bump in its orbit. Not enough to throw it off course, but enough to cause a slight judder.

Even the coffee pouring out of the machine had seemed to pause in its downward flow.

Myra blinked. Her mouth stretched into an involuntary yawn. This was the longest she had gone without disappearing into the mirror for her daily fix of slumber. Her brother and his family had left only a week ago, and she missed them dearly. As did Arjun. Or Aria now. He couldn't decide. The familiarity of his old self played tug-of-war with the novelty of his new self. The possibility that he could become someone else altogether was still an exhilaratingly new idea.

She tried to remain objective about his explorations. But in her heart of hearts, she hoped it was only a passing phase. A sudden interest in something new, something unfamiliar, for she herself often dressed in trousers and tops.

Deep down, she was utterly terrified. The world was still too insecure to tolerate any display of authenticity that was contrary to its standards.

And Arjun was such a sweet boy. He had not a sliver of aggression in him. So many girls these days were way more aggressive than her sweet boy.

That was the trouble with today's world. For aeons, it had upheld the stereotypes of docile girls and aggressive boys. People had been terrified of loud girls and ashamed of sensitive boys.

And now loud girls were celebrated whereas sensitive boys, already too quiet to begin with, have grown even quieter, unsure of their place in this world where the one who shouts the loudest for the longest is heard and all other voices are drowned in the din.

Today's world was a terrifying place for tender boys, even if nothing else about their appearance or attire or attitudes drew unwarranted flak.

A desire to spend the afternoon playing board games with Arjun tugged at her heart.

Off late, he had taken to spending more and more time by himself. She was loathe to disturb him when he was so engrossed in his life. Reading. Drawing. Practising chords on his synth. Thinking. Dreaming. Watching clouds drift and butterflies flit. Sashaying about in his frock (she ought to buy him more dresses and skirts) and admiring himself in the mirror.

The mirror!

Coffee forgotten, she ran up the stairs two at a time into their bedroom and dashed through the open door. Arjun was sitting on the bed, dressed in his pink and orange frock, looking out the window. He turned to her and smiled.

"Are you OK?" Myra asked, plonking herself beside him and trying to steady her breath.

"You won't believe what just happened."

"What happened?"

"I met Aria." He grinned.

"Aria?"

"Yes." He nodded.

"Aria, as in yourself?"

Another nod.

"I don't understand," Myra said.

"In the mirror," he explained, pointing towards the white-framed, cheap mirror that hung on the wall innocently.

Heart in throat, Myra swallowed and said, "Your reflection, you mean?"

"Hmm, yeah," Arjun said, knitting his eyebrows, the way he usually did when taking his time to choose the right words to say. Myra wished he'd hurry up and tell her what he had seen in the mirror, what the mirror had shown him. "But she's also her own person. And she took me to her home."

"Her home?" Myra tried to hold her voice steady.

"Yeah. Where she lives. Inside the mirror."

10

That night, Myra broke her first and third rules in a desperate attempt to follow the fourth. The mirror had laid bare its secrets to Arjun. Consequently, the second rule, that her sweet, tender boy shall not be made privy to its magic, was irreparably broken.

She stood in front of the mirror, uttering a silent prayer that she'd meet someone who would explain to her the magic of the mirror.

When the mirror shimmered and sparkled, she stepped into its glow, leaving behind Arjun, alone and fast asleep in their bedroom in the middle of the night.

She hadn't expected to step into the noontime meadow of her painting, yet the darkness of the world behind the mirror unnerved her quite a bit. Strange, unfriendly creatures lurked in the dark, her mother had often told her, not referring to the paranormal kind but the very real human type.

As her eyes grew accustomed to the darkness, her own bedroom appeared as a recognizable pattern of silhouettes against the pale light of the night. Everything on this side of the mirror was identical to that on the other side, except for Arjun. Her child was not here. Just as surely as she was not in her bedroom, the real one.

But someone else was. A shadow peeled itself away from the far darkness and glid towards her. Before it approached her, it drifted to the wall on the other side of the bed. With a click of a switch, the room in the mirror was flooded with light.

Myra instinctively squeezed her eyes shut in response to the unexpected explosion of light, then blinked a few times until it no longer stung.

And then she saw her. Herself. Her mirror-self. Smiling. And then the smile stretched into a yawn.

"Sorry," her mirror-self said, mid-yawn. She even sounded like Myra. Perhaps, a little more elegant.

Her pyjamas were identical to those of Myra's. The top featuring a penguin wearing a scarf and a caption that read, "Baby, it's cold outside!" and capri pants with rows of penguins sporting scarfs of different colours.

On her mirror-self, the pyjamas appeared tailor-made. Her hair was tousled but somehow she managed to pull off the messy look. It came across as chic on her. As far as Myra's messy hair was concerned, even a bird's nest would have appeared far tidier in comparison.

Every time Myra looked into the mirror for the sole purpose of appraising her appearance, she had been dissatisfied. And now, encountering her mirror-self in this mirror-world, Myra felt even dowdier than ever before.

"It's not your fault," her mirror-self said. "That's what mirrors do."

"What do mirrors do?"

"They take your beauty and stash it away, until you stop looking into them to understand how beautiful you truly are."

Myra mulled over this revelation. It made sense to her but also didn't. Like a koan. A puzzling way to ignite a realization, a spark of enlightenment.

Her mirror-self sat on the bed and beckoned to Myra to join her. Myra sat on the edge of the bed, feeling like an intruder in her own bedroom. Even her mirror-self was a distinct entity.

Her reflection bore a softness that Myra often found lacking in her own self. A nurturing gentleness. As if her mirror-self was someone who could be a very good friend to Myra.

Had the mirror taken that too from her? Or had Myra turned all her care and affection outwards, towards Arjun, sparing nothing for her own self?

"Is that the price I pay for the gift of time this mirror gives me?" Myra asked.

Her mirror-shelf shook her head. "No, that is merely the price you pay for looking into a mirror. Any mirror, not this one alone."

"That's quite a hefty price to pay for seeking one's own beauty in a mirror."

"You could look at it that way, I suppose."

"I wonder then, what price you'll make me pay for all the times I've stepped into the mirror and fallen asleep in this world."

Her mirror-self smiled. "Not me. I don't ask for anything. I am nothing more than who you are. It is the mirror that sets the rules and we abide by them."

"What are these rules? Please tell me. I must know."

"You are worried for Arjun," her mirror-self said.

Myra nodded. "I'm always worried for him," she said before she could stop herself. She was admitting, for the first time in her life, to another adult how anxiety had become her default state when it came to all matters pertaining to Arjun. "And if I'm not aware, that anxiety soars out of control and morphs into anger. Which is why I find it is so crucial for me to sleep well. To rest and heal. Leave behind one day fully before entering another."

Her mirror-self understood. "The first time you came here, you slept for half a day," she said. "Twelve hours in one go."

Myra laughed.

"Off late, you've settled to a fairly consistent eight or nine hours," her mirror-self added.

"How is it that all that time passes in this world, but when I go back to the real world, not a moment has gone by without me?"

"Like beauty, time is another element that seeps from your world into ours."

It became quite clear to Myra what this statement of fact implied. "Will that leave me with less time in the real world?"

"Yes," her mirror-self said. "The time that you gain in this world, you pay for it with time from your own life in the real world."

"How?"

"For every hour that you spend here, you give up several times as many hours of your lifetime in the real world."

"But I haven't lost any time in the real world," Myra said.

"Not yet. Because those hours are culled from the end of your life."

Realization hit Myra like a slap in the face. "Say I was

originally destined to die when I turn eighty years old. But now, because of my meanderings into this mirror-world, I may die at the age of seventy?"

Her mirror-self nodded. "I wouldn't put a precise number to it. Because no one ever knows when they'll die. But you will die sooner than you were fated to. That is the price you pay."

A heavy weight settled in Myra's heart. She put a hand on her chest and rubbed it. Words failed her.

"A mirror can only give back to you what you put into it," her mirror-self said. "Never an exact replica, but warped in some way."

11

A child of older parents, Myra had been only fifteen years old when her mother turned fifty and her father turned sixty-one.

The near-overnight decline in their health and zest for life had made Myra pray silently to whichever Gods deigned to listen that she wouldn't live a day past fifty. There was little joy in living, merely existing, without the energy and exuberance of youth, she had reasoned haughtily.

Now, having turned forty only a few months ago, Myra was as terrified of the prospect of death as Arjun had been at the age of four.

Now that she had a child, Myra no longer wanted to die at fifty. She wanted to live forever. Old enough to see Arjun grow up, marry, have babies of his own. One lifetime was not enough.

She wanted to spend countless lifetimes with her child, watch his life unfold, and hoard the knowledge of every single detail of his life, now and forevermore, just as how she had known everything about him ever since he was born—what his every coo or gurgle or cry implied, what he longed for, what hurt or scared him, and what made his heart sing.

Petrified, she started to do the math. How long had she spent in the mirror so far? How many weeks or months did all those hours add up to? How many months or years will be wrenched out of her life as a consequence?

How much longer of this life did she have? Twenty years? Ten? Will she die tomorrow? Will she die right now?

Forty-year-old single mother dies in sleep. Six-year-old son orphaned.

The captions flashed in the eye of her mind like a news ticker.

Like a prophecy. An omen. The thought terrified her. But rage quickly followed fear.

Furious with herself, Myra pushed away her blanket and marched out of the bedroom. She headed straight down to the kitchen and prepared a cup of coffee. It was three in the morning. Arjun would wake up in another two hours. And sleep was determinedly elusive.

As the coffee machine sputtered and hissed and spat out the near-black potion, Myra's frantic mind quietened. Setting aside her fearful extrapolation of the situation, she tried to recall what her mirror-self had said.

No one ever knows when they will die.

What if Myra would have lived past hundred but now she'd only live until she turned ninety? Or even eighty or seventy or sixty for that matter?

Wasn't she having a grand time with Arjun now? She shared such an easy-going, respectful bond with her child, surely a few years at the fag end of her life were worth forfeiting.

Look at her own parents now. Mother would turn seventy-five soon and Father was eighty-six years old. For all practical purposes, they were non-existent in her life. They had disowned her a decade ago when she had chosen to elope with Nick.

That she was marrying *out of caste* was deemed an act of sacrilege by her South Indian middle-class parents. She was also marrying *out of religion, out of skin colour, out of nationality,* sins from which there'd never be any redemption for her.

"You might as well marry a green alien from outer space!" her mother had shrieked.

Arjun's arrival had done little to mellow their anger, though they had condescended to chat with their only grandson on FaceTime every weekend. The sight of him sashaying about in a skirt would deal yet another blow to whatever pretence of a relationship with them she clung to.

She sipped her coffee, wishing for the first time in a long time she had a cigarette to steady her nerves. Not yet four in the morning. A little more than one hour to go before Arjun woke up and the long, long day ahead of them would begin. She was already beginning to feel resentful of his existence in her life.

No. No. No. That way lay madness all over again.

Perhaps she could drive to the nearest convenience store and buy some smokes. It would take no longer than seven minutes. But what if Arjun chose this particular morning to wake up earlier than usual only to find her gone? How would that damage and scar his psyche? Not to mention, the various child endangerment and protection laws she'd violate by this small, impulsive act.

She opened the main door and stepped out barefoot. A

blast of cold, dewy air brought her to her literal senses. Goosebumps prickled the skin on her arms. A robin trilled in the distance. The scent of clean, crisp air cleansed her lungs. The sky was a dark blue-purple, an indescribable shade of new beginnings.

She took a sip of her coffee and at once, its bitter taste was at odds with everything else around her. She stared into her mug and frowned at the beverage. A manmade concoction of substances that disrupted sleep patterns. Ever since she had been catching up on sleep in the mirror-world, her need for coffee in the real world had diminished.

Often, she reached for a cuppa out of unconscious habit, an addiction, the way a smoker lights up another stick without even thinking about it, his hands and lips automatically doing what they've learned to, what they've been trained to, despite the images of sickness and death plastered on the packets.

Come to think of it, smoking a cigarette to collect herself was hardly any different than disappearing into the mirror for a few hours of rest. The certainty of short-term pleasure was more alluring than the unpredictability of long-term safety.

It was all a crap shoot, anyway. No one ever knows when they will die. You could smoke a pack a day and live to a hundred or beyond. You could abstain from all the vices ever known to mankind yet nothing would stop an errant driver from knocking you down accidentally on your twentieth birthday.

Besides, her mirror-self had said there was no way to tell how many hours of her lifetime Myra would have to forfeit. What if for every hour she spent in the mirror, she only had to give up half an hour of her life? If there was no way to know, it all came down to what she believed, didn't it?

At least, this way she was a much better mom to Arjun and a much calmer person, kinder and gentler and more present with herself than she had ever been.

She turned back inside and poured out the rest of her coffee into the sink. Upstairs she went, quietly, and was relieved to find Arjun still fast asleep.

The sight of her sleeping child never failed to move her heart. The rise and fall of his chest with every breath, his six-year-old body lying spreadeagled, not a care in the world. For why should he worry? He had a mother whose love he was assured of.

Myra kissed him gently on his cheek, then tiptoed away from the bed and into the mirror.

Right now, it was time to sleep.

ENJOYED YOUR MOTHER'S NIGHTMARES?

Thank you for reading *Your Mother's Nightmares*!

If you loved the collection, I hope you will consider writing a short review—even a simple line or two—on the site where you bought the book.

Publishing is still driven by word of mouth, and when you leave a review it helps other readers decide this is a book worth reading. Thank you for your help in spreading the word.

You can also sign up to my monthly newsletter for updates on new book releases as well as heartfelt reflections on writing, reading, parenting and living the creative life.

Monthly Missives from The Dream Pedlar
https://thedreampedlar.com/newsletter

AUTHOR'S NOTE

Dear Reader,

I often say that motherhood has been the greatest spiritual journey I've ever set out on. Even though I began 'seeking' in my early twenties, it wasn't until I became a mother that I found the answers that made sense to me, answers to all those burning questions about life, its meaning and its purpose.

Becoming a parent brought me face to face with who I truly am, what my beliefs and conditionings are, what I truly value, and taught me to evaluate and transform how I show up in life, each day, each moment.

I hope these stories you've just finished reading empower you to meet your own parenting-related anxieties with great compassion for yourself.

To offer you more encouragement and solidarity, I've added a section titled 'Story Notes' right after this message, including personal anecdotes for each story to share a little more on the thoughts that swirled in my head and prompted me to write them.

Thank you for reading this far. I'd love to stay in touch

with you. And I hope you'd like to stay connected with me too.

I send out a monthly newsletter on the last Sunday of every month. Subscription is free.

You will be the first to hear of my forthcoming works. I also include updates on my writing life, book recommendations, free short fiction, and occasional surprises.

Thank you for staying with me this far. If you choose to accompany me further on this journey, I promise you a magical ride.

Climb aboard at https://thedreampedlar.com/newsletter!

~ Anitha Krishnan
Burlington, Ontario
Wednesday, 17 April 2024

STORY NOTES

THE PARTY ACROSS THE STREET

We first moved to Burlington, Ontario, in the spring of 2018. It was my initiation into living the suburban life in North America.

In those initial weeks and months, I was constantly taken aback by the fact that you could live right next-door to someone and yet not see them for days and weeks on end.

The windows in the living room of our townhome overlooks a small front lawn, beyond which is a private road. The other side of the road is flanked by a row of backyards of another set of townhomes.

The house directly opposite mine seemed unoccupied. They only had a short wire fence, which offered me a direct view into their backyard and kitchen window. I never saw any signs of life in there.

But strangely, their backyard was impeccably tidy in the summers. The lawn was mowed. The plants were trimmed.

I've never found out how they—whoever 'they' were—managed that.

The only rational explanation I have is that whoever came to tend to their backyard must have done so quickly and quietly when I wasn't looking (which was most of the day, by the way, in case you were wondering).

D (my child, Dhruv) was barely two years old when we moved to this neighbourhood. As a stay-at-home mom, I was constantly lonely and always worrying whether I was doing enough for my child.

I couldn't reconcile the blissful innocence of a child with the surprising ugliness the world seems to be capable of. How could one thrive in the midst of the other?

I remember when I got my driving license a few months later and began to take D to community centres and play areas farther than we could get to on bike. On one of these car journeys, The Weeknd's *Starboy* started to play on the radio.

I loved the song so much that I let it play, assuming D wouldn't understand the explicit nature of the lyrics anyway. That indeed turned out to be the case, but later I felt a pang of terrible guilt at having exposed my baby to explicit language.

My maternal brain and my wild imagination made an explosive combination in those days. I was always worried that someone would scold me for these little 'oversights' instead of giving myself a pat on the back for putting in the effort to be a conscious and peaceful (although not perfect) parent to D.

Anyhoo, the sight of the definitely empty house across the street from ours, my constant feeling of inadequacy as a parent, and the heart-rending lyrics of *Starboy* by The Weeknd fell into a magical kaleidoscope and yielded the short story you now know as *The Party Across The Street*.

(On an aside, I'm a huge fan of The Weeknd. As a contemporary artist, he is so prolific and his songs are so varied in nature, his body of work inspires me to experiment with my own writings and let each story take me wherever it wants to. He's a great inspiration to me.)

In early 2020, another neighbour said to us that that house was sold, and that the new family that had moved in had a little boy who was the same age as mine and another wee one was on the way. We were excited at the thought of a playmate right across from our home.

Only, the pandemic followed. And shortly after moving in, the family had their wire fence taken down and replaced with a tall wooden fence. Occasionally, I hear the sounds of children playing in the yard, but they disappear as quickly as they come.

I did meet the family once on a walk around the neighbourhood. And that was it. I don't think I'd recognize any of them if our paths were to cross at the neighbourhood park or the grocery store.

Perhaps one of these days I'll walk around to their front door and introduce myself. Until then, I can continue to indulge in moaning about the isolation of living in a North American suburb.

A SUITABLE COLOUR FOR A GHOST

Death is a topic I seem to explore quite often in my works of fiction.

I can't quite remember when I started to obsess over it, but I vividly recall this one evening in the early 2010s when we were living in Singapore. Abhinav (my husband) and I were out on a stroll. This was long before D's arrival into our lives.

I remember being seized by the terror of the likelihood that one of us could pass away before the other did. The thought that I could someday be the bereaved one filled me with so much fear that I turned to Abhinav and said that I didn't intend to live a single moment longer than he gets to.

In fact, I remember I wished I could become so tiny that he could carry me around in his shirt pocket wherever he went, so that we'd never have to be apart. Oh, those heady days of innocent, impractical love!

When I asked him if he'd be able to go on living in my absence, he very stoically responded in a way that meant 'Yes' without quite rubbing it in my face! At least he was honest. Always has been.

Of course, now that D is in the picture, I wish for a long, fulfilling lifetime with him and Abhinav and whoever else comes into our lives. Which means I've had to relegate all my thoughts on death to fiction.

When we were younger, my brother—who's five and a half years older than I am—used to ask my mom if she'd come and visit him as a ghost after she passed away. I remember being appalled by that idea and warned my mom very sternly to never haunt me. I must have been six or seven years old at the time.

In the past few years, we've lost many family members to illnesses or old age or accidents. We've never kept these truths away from D. This has prompted several conversations around death over the years.

Recently, D learnt to play *Amazing Grace* on the piano. His teacher explained to him that it is a slow song, usually played on sad occasions. Which brought us back to the topic of death and funerals and cremation, and I shared with D how my brother and I had reacted differently when we understood that our parents would pass away some day.

I said to D that I'd love for him to play the piano at my funeral (although I suppose I'd be cremated), and we had a fun discussion about my favourite pieces that I love to hear him play—*Für Elise*, *Alma Mater Blues* (which is a peppy number), *Spring* from Vivaldi's *Four Seasons*, and something from his several and varied compositions. The list keeps changing as he goes on to learn more and more melodies to play.

And then I exclaimed in jest, "You play these pieces so beautifully maybe I'll come back as a zombie to hear you play."

The look of outrage he gave me was hilarious!

～

MEMORY GAMES

Mommy guilt! Parental guilt! Gosh! So much of our parenting/motherhood journeys are marred by this feeling. It haunts us constantly.

Naturally, I wrote this story out of a desperate desire to remove every mistake I've made from little D's memory. It's as if something in me simply won't allow me to make mistakes when it comes to parenting, and will castigate me endlessly every time I slip up.

I had a lot to say on this topic of parental guilt—the usual sermons on how futile it is, how it only keeps us from accepting our essentially flawed and altogether human selves —but I think this article titled *Parent Guilt: A Silent Epidemic* by Robin Grille over at The Natural Child Project says it all really well.

https://www.naturalchild.org/articles/robin_grille/parent_guilt.html

The TL;DR version is that ours is the first generation of parents looking to care for our children's mental and emotional wellbeing when our own needs in these areas were likely not met.

So we're quite literally learning by doing, we are complete beginners at this, and it is grace, not guilt, that will carry us through this very arduous task.

Like my friend Xue says, we all need 'study buddies' on this lifelong learning journey!

∾

THE GOLDILOCKS ZONE

We've spent much of D's early childhood in solitude. It was the three of us, Abhinav, D and me, for the most part, what with family being so far away in India.

I used to be on several parenting groups on FaceBook, and one constant refrain was that parenting in a nuclear family setup is impossible. What we all need is a community.

I've often fantasized having a large, multi-generational family, like the ones in books and movies, where everyone looks out for each other and has each other's backs, where you know you have people you can trust and reach out to when in need.

But often we forget that these other members of this so-called 'community' are people too. People with their own opinions and beliefs, especially when it comes to raising a child. People who have expectations of us just as we too have some expectations of them in terms of behaviours and attitudes. People with whom we have relationships that need to be cultivated and managed alongside the already difficult task of parenting.

Living in a community may not be as easy and hunky-dory as we imagine it to be, especially when we're struggling with looking after a small child and any alternative to doing it all by ourselves comes across as a tempting cure-all.

I used to listen to meditation teacher Tara Brach's talks a lot in those days. One anecdote she often shared was the story of a group of porcupines, each of whom was shivering in the cold. Then they huddled together for warmth, and that indeed proved to be a successful strategy in keeping the cold at bay, except that each was inadvertently poked by the others' quills.

In essence, when we seek the warmth and support of a community, we are also vulnerable to the hurts and wounds that inevitably come from two or more people living together or in constant, close contact with each other.

I shied away from seeking much help in those days; I was in a very vulnerable state of mind, very sensitive to judgement, and I was looking for the perfect kind of support in which I'd be helped but not judged.

Maybe that was asking for too much, and in a way I too was judging the other.

Well-meaning friends would ask me to come over and watch a movie, when all I really wanted back then in those early days was to be with little D.

Talking about parenting woes with other moms sometimes ended up becoming like a competitive sport; the medal goes to whoever can prove they have it harder.

Many well-intentioned folks would give us advice with the expectation that we'd follow it; they'd feel insulted if we chose to not act on their suggestion.

The number of people who told me that I ought to put D in daycare was far too many to keep track of; it added to my guilt of choosing to be a stay-at-home mom to him.

I knew even back then, and I can say so with much confidence even now, that the child thrived and continues to thrive on having free, unstructured time. But constantly being told to make choices other than the ones I was making significantly eroded my self-trust and confidence in my ability to parent well.

My parents and Abhinav poured unconditional love on me in those days. Somehow they knew how to give me space even when I myself didn't know how to ask for it gracefully. They knew how to listen without offering advice or judgement, understanding that sometimes I just needed to talk things out loud to make sense of it all.

These are invaluable qualities they possess, and now I too try to show up in that way for the people I meet in the course of my day-to-day life.

This is really a tricky balance to find. Those FaceBook parenting groups formed my community in those days. I could spend time there as and when I needed, and switch off when I wanted space and silence.

We can't have these on-off switches when other people are involved in real life. They are human, not a random website on the Internet that we can shut off when we've had our fill.

I think of the story of porcupines a lot to help keep things in perspective when we are with extended family.

It also helps to remember that even in a nuclear family, our quills do end up poking the others and vice versa on occasion.

And finally, it really helps to remember that the Goldilocks Zone is most certainly an illusion, at least when it comes to parenting and life in general. There is no perfect way. There is no easy way. It's a very difficult task.

The best we can do is to make the most of the situation we're in, instead of wishing we had more family or less, instead of believing that the grass is greener on the other side. Life, after all, is truly not about what happens to us but about how we respond to it.

~

HIDE-AND-SEEK

If I had to choose one favourite story from this collection, *Hide-and-Seek* would be it.

Every dialogue in this tale is one I've had with D in real life. Every single one of them.

From wondering how we can get inside a book, inside a story, to referring to a small idol of Krishna as a blue person, to declaring that we come back after we die ... all these conversations happened in real life.

Once we turned to the last page of a picture book—it didn't have any text in it—and D was waiting for me to read. I realized then that he thought I was reading the story from the pictures. This was long before he fell into the words of letters and alphabets, the world of literacy.

I used to maintain a Notes app in which I diligently recorded some of the amazingly imaginative things D used to say in his younger days. I compiled them in a blog post on D's fifth birthday—titled *The Poetry of Growing Older*—when it became evident that this innocent part of himself was fast slipping away.

I share some of them here.

❧

D: I feel like the clouds are going to fall.
Me: What will happen then?
D: We will carry them on our heads.

❧

D (noticing a hole in the knee of his pyjama one morning): Why is there a hole in my pyjama?

Me: It is worn out, sweetie.

D: Do T-shirts get worn out?

Me: Yes.

D: Do people get worn out?

~

D (at the park on a very windy spring morning): Stop this windy thing, Mumma.

~

D, looks at himself in the mirror and yells, "Mumma, I found myself!"

~

D (at bedtime): Mumma, keep hugging me till tomorrow morning.

~

You can read many more of these delightful utterances on my blog.

https://thedreampedlar.com/the-poetry-of-growing-older/

~

THE GIFT OF TIME

Time becomes such a precious commodity the instant a child arrives. It feels as though there's always so much to do and so little time to get it all done. Not to mention how we all crave for deep, uninterrupted sleep.

Being a parent then becomes an excellent exercise in shedding all that's not valuable to us and guarding space and time only for the handful of things we truly cherish.

For me, I only want to spend time on D, Abhinav and writing. I don't really have any hobbies, to be honest, and I don't much care for them, except reading, of course.

Off late, I've added healthy living to the mix, now that D is close to turning eight and I do have the twin luxuries of time and lack of parental guilt to devote some time to working out and making healthier food choices than I used to.

Some elements in this story are true. We didn't have a full-length mirror at home, so whenever D wanted to look at himself from head to toe, we'd lift him up and prop him by the edge of the sink so he could take a look in the mirror above it.

We found a cheap $10 mirror at Canadian Tire one day, and put it up in D's room. One night I did see the strange lights. and hear the clicking sounds in D's room, which went away every time I switched on the bedside lamp.

D also used to love pink and purple as his favourite colours. He used to sashay about in my tunics and enjoy wearing my jewelry. In his early days at school, he was a vocal supporter of 'anybody can like any colour, anybody can wear anything'.

As was wont to happen, the opinions of the world outside have slowly been making him doubt his choices.

When he started to question himself, I once happily showed him the pictures of the singer Harry Styles wearing a skirt. (Styles is a familiar name to D as we've heard his songs on the radio quite often. *As It Was. Adore You. Watermelon Sugar.*)

We've stood by D steadfastly, often reminding him that other's opinions of him are fleeting at best and do not really matter.

He is not always convinced, and I reckon this journey of going away and coming back to his true self is something he'll have to make over the course of his lifetime.

We can only keep reminding him how amazing he is and that we love him just the way he is. It's a lesson to be learnt over a lifetime, even for us grown-ups!

MORE BOOKS BY ANITHA KRISHNAN

https://thedreampedlar.com/books/

Dying Wishes

Finalist for 2023 Rakuten Kobo Emerging Writer Prize in Speculative Fiction category

A contemporary fantasy novel weaving Hindu mythology and South Indian folklore into a quest for belonging across different worlds — the World of Mortals and the World of Gods, India and Canada, the past and the present, the world outside and the one within.

Erased from Existence

A paranormal mystery in which a fifteen-year-old is erased from the memories and perception of everyone. Trapped in oblivion, she will have to unearth and reveal long-buried family secrets to escape.

The Land of No Reflection

A fantasy tale of two sightless young women on the run from their homeland, having committed the unpardonable crime of seeing.

A Benevolent Goddess

A story of a goddess who is punished for her desire to help human beings but is unable to find salvation by any other means.

~

In Search of Leo

A fantasy tale exploring the gamut of emotions that loss and grief can stir.

~

The Mind Meddler

A short fantasy story on the games The Mind Meddler plays by sneaking thoughts into people's minds, until he meets the one person who can resist his unkind mischief.

~

Hello, Dreamer! Poems & Dreams

An eclectic collection of 100 short poems encompassing musings on the universe and its mysteries, nature and human life, my secret longings and fears, love and heartbreak, the sun and the moon, the stars and the seas, light and shadow, and joy and nostalgia.

ABOUT THE AUTHOR

Anitha Krishnan is a speculative fiction author and an award-winning poet. Her fantasy novel, *Dying Wishes*, was a finalist for the 2023 Rakuten Kobo Emerging Writer Prize in the Speculative Fiction category.

She has lived in and left pieces of her heart in many places across the world including Singapore, Australia, Canada, and most of all in her beloved birthplace, India. She presently lives in Burlington, Ontario with her husband and their cherished child.

Find more books and her blog on the writing life at
https://thedreampedlar.com.

Sign up to her monthly newsletter at
https://thedreampedlar.com/newsletter
to receive heartfelt musings, exclusive updates, book
recommendations, free fiction, and more!